A *Faithful* CHOICE

Also by Theresa Grant
Published by Create Space and Amazon.com

Hope and Desire
To Love Again
Destiny of The Wolf
Love, Passion and Hate (A Faithful Choice 2)
The Adventures of Robbie Robot and Race Moonwalker
The Sacrifice

A *Faithful* CHOICE

THERESA GRANT

A FAITHFUL CHOICE

This is a work of fiction. All of the characters, names, incidents, organizations, and dialogue in this novel are either the products of the author's imagination or are used fictitiously.

iUniverse books may be ordered through booksellers or by contacting:

iUniverse
1663 Liberty Drive
Bloomington, IN 47403
www.iuniverse.com
1-800-Authors (1-800-288-4677)

ISBN: 978-1-4917-5399-6 (sc)
ISBN: 978-1-4917-5378-1 (e)

Library of Congress Control Number: 2014920733

Printed in the United States of America.

iUniverse rev. date: 12/29/2014

Contents

DEDICATION

I DEDICATE THIS BOOK TO MY FAMILY, FRIENDS,
AND ALL OF MY FANS WHO HAVE STUCK
WITH ME, AND HAVE SUPPORTED ME WITH
EVERY BOOK THAT I HAVE WRITTEN.

Acknowledgments

Theresa's major influences have been her teachers from Long Ridge Writer's Group, Universal Class, Montgomery College in Rockville, Maryland and other published authors.

Chapter One

"Ok, Sonny, it's up to you. Me and your kid or your Aunt Virginia?" Sweat beaded Dolores' upper lip. She radiated the tension and excitement of her challenge and feared that she was going to lose. "Decide now and decide fast."

Sonny's face flushed red and then darkened. His mouth took on an unpleasant twist that contorted his ruggedly handsome face and he yelled, "Are you crazy? I'm all she's got."

Dolores felt whipsawed, watching Sonny intently, her expression baffled, alarmed. She thought of their past life together, the deep closeness that had grown between them from teenage love to the passionate love of two adults, and the compatibility they shared in every way. They loved each other once. Why didn't he love her now? Couldn't he see that she was unhappy? "I can't go on this way, Sonny, it's unbearable living here. Half the time, Virginia don't know which way is up."

"Ok, she shoots a little heroin." He lowered his voice. "Does that warrant leaving her?"

Dolores picked her way across the room, sidestepping Virginia's dope litter on the floor. "Syringes are all over the house." She met his stern expression. "She's fifty-two, should know better, and is not a good example for either of us."

He stared at her hard, his eyes piercing hers, gazing at her as if she'd lost her mind, then waving her away. "I can't leave her."

"Then get her into some program."

Virginia, listening to their conversation, rose up from the sofa, where she'd lain all night in her persistent compulsive stupor. Her speech was slurred. "Leave my boy alone,"

Dolores had to set her straight. Anger lit her eyes as she turned to face her. "Mind your own business, hag. You've interfered too often in our affairs."

Virginia swiftly rose from the sofa, her hair piled on her head like a gray mop, and her bloodshot eyes flashing. "You little parasite. Where'd you be if he hadn't married you?"

Dolores came back at her, "Not strung out somewhere on dope, that's for sure."

"You stupid little bitch." She lunged her beanpole body at Dolores.

Sonny stepped between them, escorted Virginia back to the sofa, and turned on Dolores, glaring at her with reproachful eyes and heated words. "I can't believe you. I work hard at the California Waterfront and P.F. Chang's Restaurant. Still this ain't enough for you."

Dolores stood alone, her mind congested with doubts and fears. A glazed look of despair crept over her face and, realizing that there was nothing else she could do, she wanted to say something that may force him into reality. "Ok, Sonny, if you're not man enough to do what's got to be done, I'll get a job and do it for you."

Gazing at Dolores, with hatred in her eyes, Virginia yelled, "You ain't leavin' that brat with me."

"Don't worry. I'd never leave her with a junkie."

Virginia started for Dolores again, and Sonny held onto her.

Dolores picked Michelle up and fled the house. "I've got to find a job." She was walking downtown with Michelle in her arms and passed the Holiday Inn. Something caught her eye and she turned back. Bellhops were rolling luggage for visitors checking in and out. Seems as though they're goanna' need help, she thought, stepping inside. She was directed to the manager's office and seated comfortably. Ten minutes later, a short, bald man wearing glasses appeared. He gazed at her, then at Michelle, when she started crying.

"I'm Mr. Michaela. What can I do for you?"

Dolores shifted Michelle in her seat, shoved a cookie in her hand, and hesitated a moment, thinking how best to approach this sudden interview.

When she didn't answer, he grew impatient. "How can I help you, Madam?"

Dolores attempted to bring a smile to her face when she answered, "I'm looking for work."

"Type of work?" He weighed her with a critical squint.

What an asshole, she thought and was tempted to say, up yours and leave, but held her temper. "Anything __whatever you've got."

"We need maids. Other than that, we got nothing."

Dolores accepted the job and took Michelle to work with her everyday until she had made enough money to hire a sitter, and that's when she decided to take business courses at Berkeley College.

One evening, after school, Sonny met Dolores at the door with a drink. "Happy Birthday, college girl!" He took her in his arms to dance to Earth, Wind and Fire. As the night wore on, the liquor flowed, and Sonny wanted to make love. He kissed her passionately, then gently. It was the gentleness that got her. Time rolled back, and she felt as she did when they first made love: Seventeen, on fire, groaning at the sheer wonderful pleasure of making love and experiencing pure ecstasy when they climaxed. He sat up in bed, lit a cigarette, lay back on his pillar and crossed his hairy legs and thighs.

Dolores admired his features; his face was bronzed by California sun, his teeth, even and white. She laid her head in his wide, hairy chest, placed one of his strong arms around her and smiled up at him. Thinking that she could talk to him after what had just happened between them, she asked hastily, "Ever dreamed of going to college?"

His voice broke with huskiness, "I never had enough money to go nowhere."

"You can go now. It wouldn't cost much."

He moved her away, his fingers biting deeply into the flesh of her shoulders. "Get real! How can I?"

"Get a second job," she answered, hoping to persuade him.

He quickly sat up and pounded the end table on his side of the bed. "Damn, you've managed to ruin a perfect evening." He hopped out of bed.

She whispered as she turned away, lay back and pulled the covers around her, "My mistake, thinking you'd even care to pull this family forward."

He got his clothes from the chair, where he had discarded them, dragged his trousers, and stormed out of the room.

Dolores slept alone till midnight when Sonny crept back into bed and proceeded to put his arm around her. She snatched his arm away and moved closer to the edge of her side of the bed.

The next day, everything was as before, but they were not speaking to each other. One month later, after breakfast, she felt nauseous and passed it off as nervousness, until she missed her period, and she wanted to sue someone for the failure of her birth control device. Here she was, pregnant and stuck in her situation with Virginia. When Baby James was born, she left him with the sitter and went back to work.

Several days later, Dolores had another fight with Virginia and she was ready to leave. "I'm taking this no longer, Sonny. Come with me now." Anger spilled over in her voice. "Let's get a place of our own."

Sonny gave her one of his usual looks, when he thought she wasn't making sense, and after a long audible breath, he angrily asked, "Why go someplace else? You and Virginia ought to learn how to get along."

"If you can't see the impossibility in that, there's no use in me explaining it to you. I'm out of here."

Dolores got a room at the Holiday Inn and paid the baby sitter to come there. One day, while cleaning the rooms, she happened to glance at the morning paper. Her stepfather's picture was in the obituary section. "Mama Kate must be frantic," she murmured, and hurried to the phone to call her. What was she going to say? They had not spoken in three years. Nevertheless, she had to see her. She dialed the number and Mama Kate answered on the first ring.

"It's Dolores, Mama."

"Thought you were dead," Mama Kate said, sounding distressed and sarcastic.

Dolores took a deep, painful breath to prevent an argument, and tried to sound sympathetic. "Sorry about Jake."

"Are you? That's a switch."

"I mean it Mama, I didn't hate him. Not even after__" She stopped, again not wanting to argue. "I'm married, Mama. You've got two grandchildren. May I come over?"

"Come ahead," she said as if she didn't care one way or the other.

Dolores took the children from the sitter and drove to Mama Kate's. When she pulled into her driveway, she was tending her flourishing garden.

She took one look at her grandchildren, wiped the sweat from her smooth, deep suntanned face and smiled, revealing alabaster dentures with a gold tooth. The sight of two beautiful children suddenly overwhelmed her. She called to them, "Come here my sweetie pies."

Baby James, just learning to walk, waddled along behind Michelle, giggled and fell upon Mama Kate's breast. They clung to her, flattening her breast, which seemed to spread from her chest to her waist, and as she wrapped her arms around them, her cotton sundress strained against her stout round hips. She set the children down and gazed at her tall, lithe daughter whose skin glowed in deep shades of golden tan under the bright sun. "Come inside outta' this sun."

Dolores and her children followed Mama Kate into the house, and she got her to talk about her life, away from home, and she ended up telling her everything about her marriage, about Virginia and Sonny's refusal to leave Virginia. "I was living on the street until Sonny took me home to live with him; remembering that night when she first met him at a dance at the MLK Youth Service Center. Sonny came over and asked her for a dance, and she looked up at him, a huge, six foot boy, just a little taller than she, with deep tan skin, a strong square featured face, closely-cropped black hair and sideburns that gave him an air of strength. "You know what you do to me?" he whispered, his hot breath penetrating her inner ear.

She met his gaze and the suggestive gleam in his eyes. "Let me guess. You're talking about sex, right?" Her voice was low and silky.

He didn't answer just smiled and tightened his arms around her waist, and drew her closer to the point where their bodies seemed as one. They talked and he found out that she had no place to stay.

"Let's get outta' here. Got a place you should check out." He took her home and asked Virginia to let her stay. Virginia was nice until she came home, one day, and found Sonny and her making love. "I was seventeen and pregnant when Virginia made us get married."

"I wouldn't have married such a no-good man," Mama Kate said with a smirk on her face.

Her words were barbed and hurtful. Anger swept across Dolores' face and she couldn't hold her tongue. "Get off it, Mama, Daddy left you and mean Jake used you."

Mama Kate's eyes took on a pained look as if someone had stuck her with a knife.

Dolores didn't relent, but continued, "He was skipping work, in bed watching television all day, while you were working."

Denial flew from Mama Kate. "You're lying. Working at Sokol's Furniture store ruined Jake's back."

"Hah! He fooled you," Dolores retorted, in cold sarcasm and laughed. "He wasn't hauling furniture. Most likely humping some woman."

Her eyes darkened with pain and she said, "That's always been your problem, Dolores, a smart mouth."

That didn't stop Dolores, and she thought while they were rehashing old truths, she may as well declare another. "You never believed Jake was coming onto me."

Fire now burned in Mama Kate's eyes and she lashed out. "You were a liar then and you're one now. Didn't I whip you enough?"

"Oh, you did!" She exclaimed, tears welling her eyes, remembering that night when Jake came into her room, held her down and kissed her neck with his wet lips. His breath smelled like a pigsty and she wanted to puke, instead she bit his face. He yelled and let go of her, and she ran to Mama Kate. When she told her what had happened, she whipped her with a belt. "Why didn't you comfort and shield me, Mama?"

"Don't pass the blame, Dolores. You were a problem child. You know it. I could never get through to you."

"Did you try?" Her voice quivered. "It was humiliating and a deflated feeling. When you brought Jake home, I knew he was trouble."

Mama Kate waved a hand as if to shoo the idea of Jake being a threat out of her mind. "I needed a husband, and you, a father. You should've been happy 'stead of running away."

"What else could I do?"

"You ought not have married. If you had to live with Sonny and that dope head, why didn't you keep your legs crossed?"

"It happened. Ok? Life was rough on the street, but I'd have come back had I know Jake had died."

Mama Kate gazed at her with disgust. "That's just like you, Dolores."

She held her tongue, avoiding her mother's penetrating eyes. Here she was arguing with her and in the house she thought she would never see again. She apologized. "I'm sorry, Mama, I didn't mean to sound nasty and hateful."

"I'm sorry, too, if I hurt your feelings. After all, you are my daughter."

After their tempers had cooled, they called a truce, and Dolores and her children stayed all day with Mama Kate before going back to the Holiday Inn. The phone was ringing when she entered the door. Dolores answered and the familiar voice sent a delightful shiver of wanting through her body.

"You win," Sonny said, in a low sugary tone. "I miss you, babe. I see your face in my dreams. I feel your body next to mine. I smell your perfume in the bed covers."

Reluctantly, she admitted to herself that this man was in her blood. She bit her bottom lip and a cry of relief broke through her lips as she confessed, "Every night before I get to sleep, all I can think of is you."

"I'm leaving town tomorrow. Come with me."

Her mind was a crazy mixture of hope and fear. A flicker of apprehension coursed through her. In her heart she had always been afraid that her family would be separated. The thought tore at her insides. "What about the kids?"

"We can't take them till we're settled. Leave them with your mama."

"I never been without them nor they without me."

"You wanted me to leave Aunt Virginia. I've done it. I'll wait for you at the airport."

She hung up and fear clutched her heart. She was his. He knew it too. There was no way she was going to let him leave without her. Mama Kate would take care of the kids and they could join her and Sonny later.

The next morning, Dolores drove the children to Mama Kate's, after persuading her to let them stay, convinced that in the long run, it would be worth the sacrifice of being parted from them.

Mama Kate was on the front porch when Dolores drove in the driveway and ushered the children out of the car.

"Lands sake, you've brought enough clothing." She took two large nap sacks from the car. "How long you plan staying?"

"A couple of weeks." Dolores wasn't sure, but she couldn't explain it to Mama Kate without her thinking that she was running off and leaving them. "Thanks, Mama." She rushed outside and whipped the car onto the street.

Sonny was waiting at the Oakland International Airport. He was frowning and pointing to his watch. "What took you so long? Hurry!"

They boarded the Delta noon flight to Chicago, and after landing, took a limousine to the Hyatt Regency. "Look, babe." He threw open the doors to their suite. "How's this for class?"

"It's beautiful" And it was. The blue carpet and wallpaper with borders matched the spreads and draperies. Gleaming Mahogany furniture, two consoles and a built-in bar appealed to her. It was more than she had imagined.

They got settled and ordered room service. "When was the last time you had a steak this thick?" He licked his lips. "Good huh?" He finished eating, slid out of his pants and sat on the bed in his briefs. He thrust one leg over the side of the bed and gazed over at her with lust. "Come here."

Dolores got in bed. His arms curved around her, and she nestled close to him. He gently stroked her back and whispered, "Foxy lady. Sexy babe."

His voice lulled her to sleep, and when she awoke, it was dark. She flicked the night switch. Sonny had left a note. "Got business. I'll be back. Order some champagne."

From that night on, she stayed alone in the hotel while Sonny went out with associates to conduct business. Dolores wasn't as happy as she had expected. During those long, lonely nights, she became homesick and longed to see her children. One phone call, she told herself. I have to see how they're doing. Mama Kate answered and Dolores heard Michelle crying. Then Baby James started, and Mama Kate was trying to quiet them. "Hush y'all. Talk to your mom."

Michelle listened to Dolores' promise to come and get her and Baby James, and she stopped crying. When Dolores had finished talking, she couldn't hold back her tears, and she was still crying when Sonny came home. "What's up?" He gazed at her as if she had lost it.

"I called the kids," she said drying her eyes. "They miss us."

"Aw, come on, babe. They'll be fine. Order some champagne. Business was great."

"What's this job, Sonny?" She eyed him suspiciously.

A shadow of annoyance crossed his face as he answered, avoiding her eyes. "Selling."

Not believing him, she questioned him further. "Selling what?"

"Hardware. I'm getting good at it."

Dolores laughed. Joy bubbled in her laugh and shown in her eyes, and she became hopeful. "Does this mean we can go get the kids?"

He ran his hands nervously through his hair and said, irritably. "Not yet. I need a couple more weeks."

All pleasure left her in that instance. They'd been there three weeks already. Dolores thought she had better do something to hurry things along. "I can work." She viewed the want ads. "I'm here all day doing nothing."

"Whatever," he said, with little attention, and dialing room service. When the champagne arrived, he drank it all and fell asleep.

Early the next morning, Dolores got dressed, went outside and hailed a taxi. "Marshall Fields Department Store," she told the driver. She got out, hurried inside and felt exhilarated mingling with the crowd of shoppers. This store is fabulous, she thought, going to the employment office. A short, stout woman peered at her over large, black-rimmed eyeglasses. "Have you any experience?" she asked, scrutinizing her head to toe.

Dolores became uneasy under this scrutiny and her nerves tensed. Anxiety sputtered through her and she clenched her hands until her nails entered her palm. Hold on, she told herself. You need this job to bring the family together. She developed a stronger guard and answered, "I've worked three years in a hotel."

The woman gave her a long, cold stare and said, "I'll give you a try. Report here tomorrow. Eight a.m."

Dolores left the store feeling self-confident and proud. When she arrived at the hotel, Sonny was gone. He returned, later that night, in a jovial mood. He took her in his arms and danced around the room. "Let's do the town. Wear that dress with the split up the leg."

I'll be ready in two seconds," she said shedding her clothing and heading for the shower. Fifteen minutes later, she slipped into a sleek, red dress, stepped into her black patent pumps, ran the comb through her hair, strode into the room and paraded in a modeling stance before Sonny. His catlike eyes watched her desirably as her curly, raven hair bounced gently around her shoulders, her shapely, slim legs moving in unison with the swaying of her curvaceous hips.

"Miss D," his deep, baritone voice said. "You're goanna' knock them dead tonight."

Her face broke into a dazzling smile and she felt happy, light hearted and carefree.

"We'll eat at the Rooftop Restaurant. Then it's onto the town for dancing and anywhere your heart desires," he said, kissing her.

Dolores proudly held his arm as they rode the elevator to the restaurant. They were given a table for two with a beautiful view of the city. Sonny studied the menu for a moment then asked, "What's the catch of the day?"

"Catfish," the waiter answered.

"Naw, bring me a thick T-bone, baked potato, and broccoli." He turned to Dolores. "Give him your order, babe. Spare no expense."

"I'd like the Catfish, grilled lightly, no butter, please."

"Yes, ma'am, anything to drink?"

Sonny interrupted, "Bring two glasses of your best Chardonnay."

"White Zinfandel," Dolores said, smiling through her teeth. She stared at Sonny. "What's your problem? You know I don't like Chardonnay."

His face wrinkled with a scowl. "You got the problem, babe. I'll show you later."

The waiter returned with the drinks. Sonny took his drink and held it to Dolores' lips. "Taste this."

She resisted. "No."

"C'mon," he insisted, his voice firm. "Just one sip."

She stiffened and took a sip. "Ugh. It's strong!"

"Sure. Everything strong makes you feel good."

I can feel good another way, thank you," she replied, wiping her lips.

He ran his hands up her thigh. "I'll take care that later."

She slapped his hand. "Behave. Somebody might see you."

"So what? They want the same."

She laughed and shook her head. "Not everybody thinks of sex in a restaurant."

"Yes they do. Look at "Big Daddy" in the corner," he pointed to a heavy-set customer seated with a pretty companion.

They laughed, finished dinner, then went outside and Sonny led her to a red Corvette.

Dolores' eyes widened. She jumped into the car and ran her hand over the red leather, bucket seats. "Where did you get this car?"

"It's a rental, but a taste of what you can expect in the future. We travel in style." He sped off, testing the speed and came to a screeching halt when he neared the nightclub. He parked near the Ambassador East Hotel. They got out and headed for the Buttery Discotheque Nightclub. They were seated and Sonny ordered drinks. Dolores was having fun until Sonny left to use the phone, and she sat alone almost thirty minutes before he returned.

"Where were you?" She raised her voice.

He flopped in the seat beside her and stared at her, his eyes strong with anger. "Don't ask me about my business. Here, put this in your purse."

Dolores took the box and shook it. "Is this a watch?"

"Never mind," he whispered through clenched teeth. "Put it away. Hold the keys while I refresh your drink." He came back with the drink and she sipped it until the glass was empty. A few seconds later, she started blinking her eyes, her heart palpitated, and she broke out in a cold sweat. She tugged his sleeve. "I'm sick."

"Yeah, you're starting to turn pale."

"I'm coming down with something. I feel dizzy."

He helped her out of her seat. "C'mon."

"My stomach is burning and I feel nauseous." She jerked away from Sonny and ran to the ladies' room, barely making it to the toilet before she vomited. Fear crept inside of her and ugly thoughts crowded her mind, as she sat beside the toilet. Did Sonny put something in her drink? She got up and walked, swaying back to her seat to find Sonny wedged between two burly cops. "What's going on?"

They said nothing, cuffed Sonny's hands behind him and led him out to the police car. She ran outside to the Corvette, threw her purse on the floor in the back seat and followed them. "I have to know where they're taking him," she muttered, with conflicting emotions coursing through her.

The cops stopped at the third precinct, and Sonny was unloaded at gunpoint. She hurried inside.

"You're making a mistake."

One of the officers turned on her. "Who're you and what's your role in this?"

Before she could answer, he said, "We'd better take you in, also." He hustled her in with Sonny.

"You don't handle her that way, you ____" A baton across his back painfully cut off Sonny's words.

"Never mind. Where's the stuff?"

"Stuff?" Sonny asked, sweat running down his face.

"The heroin, smart-ass and don't lie." He hit Sonny again.

Dolores screamed, "Stop! You're hurting him."

A policewoman entered, twisted Dolores' arm and threw her in a chair. Dolores' breath caught in her throat. Her mind was racing with indignation and embarrassment.

Sonny held out and wouldn't admit to anything no matter how hard they hit him. "Let me call my lawyer," he demanded, and moved toward the phone. He made the call and after talking on the phone for five minutes, an hour later, She and Sonny were out of there. Sonny took the box out of her purse and handed it to a man he claimed was his lawyer. Then he took her back to their hotel.

Dolores was trembling. Tension made her temples ache and she felt dizzy. "I was scared. I could have had a record."

"C'mon, babe." He held her gently. "I'd never let that happen."

"Tell me the truth, Sonny, was heroin in that box?"

"Naw!" He lied and formed tight lips. "Those monkeys were fishing, trying to pin something on me."

They went to their suite and Sonny pulled her into his arms. "I'm still afraid." She laid her head to his chest.

"Relax," he crooned, and started singing, "Angel. You're my angel."

The words of the song and Sonny's soothing touch washed over her and she snuggled in his chest. He stroked her hair, kissed her temples, then her lips. She drifted deeper into the spell woven around her and she clung to him for a long while.

They were taking their clothes off. He pushed her down on the sofa, handling her roughly, touching her breast with his lips, pressing his lips between the folds, exploring with lips and tongue, and holding her nipples with his tongue. Then with light strokes of his tongue, tasted her all over.

Shock and delight pulsed through her and she shivered as he slid his hands between her legs, parting them. "Do you want this?"

A helpless gasp escaped her throat, and then she moaned and answered, "Yes," pushing herself underneath him.

They made love until each felt their own wave of pleasure. They fell apart, and he swiftly got up. "I've got to go out."

"What's this, Sonny? You've just got out of jail. Now you're going out this time of night?"

"Got to take care of the mess I'm in. I'll be back later."

She pressed against him and rubbed his stomach. "Don't go."

"Don't worry." He gently pushed her aside, slid out the door and called back to her, "Everything will be fine."

"What a bone head," she muttered and got ready for bed.

Later that morning, Dolores went to her job at Marshall Field. In all the confusion last night, she didn't get to tell Sonny about her job. She was assigned to the loungewear department. Several hours later, she was sorting delicate sheer apparel at her counter when a distinguishing looking gentleman approached her.

Dolores kept her gaze on him. "What a good-looking man. His features were sharp: strong jaw line, deep set hazel eyes, thick eyebrows, salt and pepper hair cut into an English Squire haircut connecting to a slim beard and mustache. He's so sexy, she thought and smiled at him.

"I'd like someone to model these items," he said, in a deep baritone voice.

His voice sounded, like a deep base horn as she stared into his dark brown eyes. "The floor manager can help you with that, sir." She dialed the code number for Mr. Bernard.

When he appeared they talked for a minute and he beckoned to her.

She hurried over and he asked, "Would you model Mr. Velasco's selections? He's an important customer."

Dolores was startled. Why would he ask her? "I've never modeled anything, sir."

"Don't matter. Just try them and let him look."

She was reluctant, but she needed the job. She took the apparel and headed for the dressing room. There were a dozen pairs of silk pajamas, Peignoir sets, slips and corsets of different colors. "I refuse to wear these slips and corsets," she mumbled, removing her clothes and getting into the pajamas. A few minutes later, she came out and did a few turns in front of Velasco, and over the course of an hour, she had modeled everything except slips and corsets.

"That'll do, thank you," Velasco said. "I'll take everything."

Dolores made a deep sigh of relief, had everything wrapped and handed the bags to a tall, dark chauffeur, who was standing by.

Velasco handed her a hundred dollars. "Thanks for your help."

Dolores gaped at the money and handed it back to him. "No, sir, it's my job."

"You've earned the money." He shoved it into her pocket.

Dolores watched him walk away. He's nice. Classy. Not like the men she knew.

That evening, when she got home, Sonny was dressing to go out. "Where you been?" he asked in a nasty tone.

"I have a job," she said happily. "Didn't get a chance to tell you last night."

"Well, ain't that sweet," he said sarcastically, mimicking a woman's voice.

"Why are you going out now?" She pulled at him.

"Business. Don't concern yourself. I'll return when I return."

"Dolores planted herself on the sofa and looked at television. Later, she prepared what she was going to wear to work the next day, and then went to bed.

The next morning, she got to the store early. Before lunchtime, Mr. Velasco returned to her counter.

Her smile widened. "Back so soon?"

"Not here to buy," he answered, gazing at her. "I've come to offer you a job."

"Me?" She gasped and her eyes widened.

"You," he said, looking serious. "Let's have lunch and talk about the job."

The ache in her tired feet eased a little, but a new one started somewhere inside her heart, and she became afraid. He wanted to hire her? Suppose she couldn't live up to his expectations? The thought blew her mind, but something in his voice pulled her, and she followed him outside. His chauffeur drove up in front of them, Dolores reached for the door and he quickly put his hand on the handle.

"Let me get that," he said, opening the door and helping her inside.

I could get used to this man, she thought. She shouldn't and she wouldn't, but she could.

They went to Biggs Restaurant on the near north side of town. Sitting across the table from him didn't feel natural at first, but when she caught his gaze, she forced herself to relax.

"I'm happy you came to lunch with me," he said, not taking his eyes from hers.

"I couldn't refuse this nice offer, Mr. Velasco."

"Please, call me Leonard," he insisted, taking the menu and acting pleased with himself.

Dolores let him order for her. They were eating and discussing business. "Don't suppose you've heard of Velasco's?"

"No. I'm new in the city. Berkeley, California is my home town."

"I knew there was something different about you." He smiled and gazed at her for a long moment, as if he were studying her, not noticing the change in her expression.

"Different?" She felt insulted.

He dropped his smile and hurried to clarify his statement. "There' a fresh, modest air about you, I haven't seen around this town."

"Is that good or bad?"

He laughed and patted her hand. "Believe me it's good. How tall are you?"

"Five-six."

"Have you ever considered modeling?"

New and unexpected warmth surged through her and sent her pulse throbbing. "No. I went to school for business and computer science."

"You'd make a great model." He reached over and took hold of her shoulders. "Lovely skin, a gorgeous figure." He turned her chin to the left. "You're the ideal height to become a model."

"You make me sound fascinating," she said, not taking him seriously.

"You could be. Do you like excitement?"

"Never thought much about excitement. I just want to be somebody."

"Work for me. You'd be one of a hundred and fifty models. I'm expanding in Paris."

"Sounds exciting." Her smile broadened with approval. "But I know nothing about modeling."

"You can learn," he said, trying to persuade her.

Dolores was shaking her head as he continued, "Two hundred dollars a day. That's more than I pay the others."

She stopped shaking her head. The idea had begun to appeal to her, and she thought about her children, and then Sonny. He had been a great disappointment. She would be crazy not to take this man's offer. "Ok," she sang with delight. "What can I lose?"

They finished eating and he took her back to the store. "Here's my phone number. Call if you have any questions."

After work, Dolores was bursting with excitement. When she got to the hotel, she rushed inside and froze. "What are you doing with that gun?"

He jerked her arm and held her against him. "Shut up! They'll hear you."

"Who?" She asked, trying to catch her breath.

Before he could answer, a squadron of men burst through the door. "Don't move," one of them yelled, flashing his badge. "Sonny Brown, you're under arrest for possession and dealing drugs."

Dolores gaped at them in shock. Then she swallowed hard the lump that grew in her throat that was taking her breath away, and she tried to think of something to say, but chocked back a cry. Frightened, electrified, hearing the sound of her heart thumping in her ears erratically, till finally she was able to speak. "Sonny, tell them they are wrong."

Sonny's eyes narrowed, darkened, his face twisted into a terrible scowl. "Wise up, babe, how'd you think we were paying for all this?"

Then her worse nightmare began. Sonny grabbed her without warning, pulling her back, and lifting her off her feet. "Back off or I'll kill her." He backed her toward the door.

Her face went pale white. Sonny's voice in her ear sounded mean, menacing, scary, and not like that of the man who had said that he loved her. Now he was squeezing her chest tighter. "Throw your guns on the floor."

Dolores quivered in outrage and pain as she asked, "How could you do this to me? The mother of your children."

Sonny didn't answer. He wasn't in a position to listen to her objections. "We're leaving."

One trooper started to rush Sonny and he held the gun to Dolores' head.

"I'll blow her brains out. I mean what I say."

"Cool it, men," the officer in charge said. "Let them leave. We'll catch him later."

Sonny pulled Dolores along like a rag doll until he got her to his car. His breathing labored, he tossed her into the passenger's seat.

Then she got angry. "You dirty bastard."

"Shut your mouth," he snarled, spit foaming in the corners of his mouth. "I couldn't let them take me."

"What about me? I could have been killed."

"Quit squawking! You're here in one piece ain't you?" He took off, pressing the accelerator all the way to the floor.

Dolores felt a hot flush of fury rising within her. Her eyes blazing, she faced him furiously. "To think I left the kids for you, an evil, no good, bum. You're worse than Virginia and not worth the hair on my kids' head."

Sonny paid her no attention. Just kept speeding. "Let me outta' this car," she yelled, shoving against his face with her left hand, then clawing his flesh with all the strength she had within her. The car careened toward the dividing line and hit a stop sign. When he backed up, Dolores reached for the door, her fingers tipped the latch and she tumbled out onto the street. Sonny sped off, peering back at her through the mirror, and she gave him the finger. She went back to the hotel, washed her bruises, and called Leonard. "How soon can I start work?"

"Dolores? I didn't recognize your voice.

"It's me." She began to cry.

"What's wrong?"

She told him everything.

"You could have been killed." He sympathized. "You'd do better to divorce that bum."

"You're right. But first, I've have to go home for my kids."

"The job is in New York. I'll have an apartment ready for you when you get there."

"Goodbye and thanks." She packed her clothes and went to the airport where she waited for a morning flight. While she waited, she thought about her children. After being away six months, she hadn't known, hadn't grasped the full implication of what she had done to them till now, and she prayed that it wouldn't leave a lasting scar on their memory. When Dolores arrived, Mama Kate saw her through the window and opened the door. They gazed at each other.

Then Mama Kate said, "You look like hell." Her mouth was pulled tautly, but she observed the despair, the hurt and the bruises on her face.

Dolores waited for the worse lecture of her life, knowing she deserved everything Mama Kate would say to her. "I've been a fool and too naïve to heed your warnings."

"Looks like you've learned a lesson. Come in. Your young ones are napping."

Dolores couldn't hold back the tears. She buried her face in Mama Kate's shoulder and wept bitterly. For the first time, since she was a child, her mama put her arms around her and cradled her.

Dolores was happy to be back with her children. It was obvious that they were happy to see her. They jumped all over her, laughing and kissing her. That morning, she prepared breakfast for her children, and stared out of Mama Kate's window. The sun was rising. It was going to be a beautiful day. Realizing how blessed that she was, she gave each of her children a kiss.

The next day, after telling Mama Kate about her job offer, she packed their clothes, went to the airport and took a flight to New York. Leonard met her at Kennedy International. Dolores introduced her children.

Leonard laughed and shook their hands. "I've ordered a car for you, Dolores. Wait till you see your apartment."

The heavy lashes that shadowed her cheeks flew up and her voice rose in surprise. "A car?"

He winked and said, "You'll be more accessible with wheels."

"Pinch me, please. I want to make sure I'm not dreaming."

He laughed and pinched her. "You're not dreaming."

They rode through Central Park and Dolores and her children were happy. Then they arrived at her apartment on the east side of Manhattan.

"Herman will take your bags. Let's get the children inside."

When they stepped off the elevator and into her apartment, Dolores flipped. "It's beautiful. I love blue and gray," She felt the satin draperies at one of the large windows in the living room, and headed toward the bedrooms. "Brass poster beds? It's everything I've seen in the House Beautiful Magazine."

"Come see the kitchen. I hope you like white. My decorator swore it's the in-thing."

"This apartment must cost a pretty penny." She sat in one of the chairs at the white oak dining table.

"You'll make enough money, as my number one model, to meet the payments."

"What have I done to warrant this lavish apartment and Job?"

"I liked you from the beginning. You have potential to make a lot of money for me. But I want to warn you about one part of the business."

Oh, here it comes, she thought, I knew it had to be a catch to everything. She held her breath and asked, "What's my job?"

"Don't be alarmed." He gazed at the expression on her face. "My models sometime go out with customers, but I'd rather that you didn't." He had shown her right then and there that he was smitten with her.

Air expelled her lungs. "Maybe I'm wrong, but do you expect me to be more than a model? If so, I don't want any part of this."

"No. I'm sorry if I gave that impression. Dating the customers is bad for the business."

"I have two kids to care for and I don't date."

"Ok. I'll explain everything tomorrow, but I want you and the children to have dinner with me tonight."

Leonard left and after she had gotten over some of her fascination for the apartment, she phoned Mama Kate to tell her the good news.

"You sure that man's not a dope peddler?"

"Mama please, I've been through all that. You think I'd get caught in that nightmare again?"

"How you know? Most of them tell you anything."

"He's a respectable business man, Mama, and he seems a little lonely."

"Be careful. You know how you are in choosing men."

"Don't rub it in, Mama. I have to go. Talk to you later." When she finished talking with Mama Kate, she and the children got dressed to have dinner with Leonard. An hour later, Herman came to get them. They climbed into the long black Cadillac, and after an hour's ride to the suburbs called Terry Town, they rode through a winding drive that seemed to be a maze before the house came into view.

Dolores was impressed. Never has she seen a house like this. There were tall columns across the front, a veranda on the second floor between the columns and six windows each side of the veranda. Lush green foliage and beautiful evergreen trees surrounded the house. They got out of the car and entered the foyer, and then into a spacious living room with French furniture that sat on a beautiful Persian rug. Dolores stood mesmerized in the doorway. "How many rooms have you got here?"

"Fifty-two. Want a tour?'

"You know that I do."

Leonard walked over to the blue velvet draperies, separating the foyer from the living room, and yanked on a long silk tasseled cord. Within minutes, a tall, dark woman with a large chignon, and dressed in a maid's attire, hurried into the room. "You rang, sir?" she asked in a heavy alto voice.

"Hattie, show Ms. Brown the house."

Yes, sir. Come, Ms."

Dolores followed Hattie up the staircase that curled up to the third floor. They stepped into the first room, which was a library with walnut shelves that reached the ceiling and lined all four walls of the room. Four round walnut tables sat next to two soft leather high-backed chairs. The floors were highly polished oak wood. Silk taffeta draperies of gold with bronze tiebacks of thick braided rope adorned the windows.

"Sure love the colors and beautiful paintings," Dolores said.

"Mr. Velasco brought them from Paris," Hattie explained, and opened the door to the last bedroom on the second floor. "This here's Mr. Velasco's bedroom."

Dolores stepped into the room and her breath caught in her throat as she imagined Leonard lying in the king-sized bed that was surrounded by large mahogany posters, reading under sparkling crystal lamps, and drinking his favorite wine. Dolores perched on the blue velvet chase lounge and reached down to feel the plush, blue carpet. "Luxurious," she said and sighed.

They came back to the first floor and entered the room that had a bowling alley, then one filled with exercising equipment of all makes and sizes and an indoor pool. Hattie led her to the kitchen. "Mr. Velasco restored this kitchen __modern appliances," she said, pointing to the refrigerator, double oven and dishwasher that were installed in the wall.

They ended the tour and joined Leonard and her children in the dining room. Two tables had been set with a standing rib roast, string beans with almonds, Caesar's salad, chocolate mousse, strawberry ice cream cake, punch for the children and White Zinfandel wine for the grown ups. They finished dinner and Leonard talked about the business. They had more wine, and then he started telling her about himself. "My family was poor till my Mom's father died and left us his fur business. My Grandfather was Native Alaskan. He started trapping furs as a boy."

"Interesting life." She regarded him with somber curiosity. "Tell me more."

"When Grandfather got enough money, he came to America. He raised Mink and Sable, married my Grandmother and left the business to my Mom."

Dolores sat across the table from him, studying his facial features and listening to him talk. When he smiled, she thought his teeth to be like the brilliance of pearls, his skin smooth as honey and his eyes the color of hazel nuts. His thick eyebrows and, salt and pepper hair gave him a distinguishing look. She couldn't move her eyes from his as he continued to talk about his business.

"Mom died and I became heir. My dream is to make the business bigger, better than its ever been." He stopped talking and his quick responsive smile brought her back to reality. "I'm boring you, aren't I?" He squeezed her hand. "Tomorrow, I'm giving you some modeling lessons. You'll make a lot of money for me."

They said good night and she and the children were driven back to her apartment. Her thoughts were of tomorrow, and making a good impression.

Chapter Two

Dolores arose early. This would be her first day on the job. I have to make a go of this position, she told herself. It's vitally important to my kids and to me. She hurriedly got dressed and left for the store. Less than half an hour later, she parked her red Honda and stood outside Velasco's on fifth and Madison Avenue. Her mind was racing with the thought of being in the Big Apple, on her own, and working for Leonard.

She went in and took the elevator to the third floor. When she stepped off the elevator, a short, dark, bearded man approached her. "You must be Mrs. Brown." He extended his hand. "Bob Green, the coordinator. Welcome."

Dolores followed him down a long hall to a big dressing room with stalls. "Look around. Familiarize yourself with the place. He shook his head as he talked. "Hope you like working here. See you around."

Dolores didn't know whether he was saying hope you do or don't like it, but she managed a smile and said, "I'm sure I will."

The first day on the job was long. Many buyers came into the store and she was on her feet all day. Going home was equally taxing. The streets were jammed packed at rush hour. It took her almost an hour to get home, and when she walked into the living room, she kicked her shoes off and lay on the sofa, wondering if everyday would be like today.

Michelle entered and sat beside her. "Time for dinner, Mommy."

"Where is your sitter?"

"Rochelle is getting ready to leave."

"I forgot about her hours." She sat up. "I've an idea. Why don't we fix hamburgers and fries?"

"Oh, yummy. I will take the patties out of the refrigerator."

Dolores followed her to the kitchen where James was seated at the table and reading a book. "Make yourself useful." She handed him three lemons. "Make lemonade."

They each finished what they were preparing. "Now, we wait for the food to cook. Wasn't working as a team fun?"

"Yes, Mommy," they said in unison.

After seeing how they worked, she thought establishing a few rules for everyone wasn't bad. After all, they weren't babies any longer. They should learn to be independent, and the sooner the better. "After tonight, let's make a pact. Everyone helps around here like tonight."

They slapped each other's palm and agreed. They equally shared in clearing the table after dinner and before going to bed.

Dolores had been working for Leonard for two months. The other models were jealous of her. When she was dressing to leave, they began whispering about her and as she left the dressing room, Julienne bumped her. "Aw, excuse me. I didn't mean to hurt boss's little pet."

Throwing her head back and placing her hands on her hips, Dolores snapped, "I'm no one's pet." She strode toward the door.

"Bosses' pet," Julienne sang, following her. "Everything and anything she wants."

All of the other models started laughing, and then chimed in. "Yeah, and you get to go out with bossy," they said, continuing to taunt her.

"Bat those big brown eyes and he comes running," Julienne said. "We work out tails off and he don't give us nothing."

"Don't blame me if Leonard doesn't spend time with y'all. I don't make the rules around here." She pushed passed Julienne and bumped the others on her way out.

They all grunted and went into the outer shop.

When Dolores was about to leave, Leonard phoned her. "Hi, gorgeous, what about dinner?"

"Sounds great. What did I do to merit such treatment?" She asked, remembering what Julienne and the others had said about her.

He let her know how he felt about her without scaring her away. "I like the way your eyes light up when you're happy, and that makes me happy."

"I bet you say that to all your models," she said, teasing.

"No, Dolores, you're the only one. Herman will come for you."

A rush of pink stained her cheeks and she cleared her throat pretending not to be affected.

It was nine-thirty when Herman drove up outside the shop. All the models stopped what they were doing to look out of the shop's window as Herman opened the car door for Dolores. Herman drove through Central Park and Dolores began to hum and enjoy the scenery. "I love this spark. It's alive with diversity."

"Yes, ma'am. Full of joggers, muggers and panhandlers trying to cop a buck."

Dolores ignored what he said and continued, "Most of all, I love the trees, green grass, and the lakes."

Herman laughed and said, "You love the park, period." He stopped in front of the mansion and let her out before parking in the garage. Leonard was waiting at the door.

"Hi, beautiful," he said, his eyes raking boldly over her.

Dolores noticed that he was watching her intently and there was a tingling in the pit of her stomach as she tried to throttle the dizzying current racing through her. He was ten years her senior. What she was feeling was no more than what she thought would be a daughter's feeling for her daddy.

Leonard came over, took her hand and brought her to a seat on the sofa next to him. "I've got a surprise for you."

"What is it? What?" She waved her hands in the air like a little girl.

"How would you like to be my coordinator?'

"You mean it?" Her eyes misted over and she threw her arms round his neck and kissed him.

"Wow! I should have told you sooner." He enjoyed her sudden enthusiasm. "Later, I'll brief you, but now, let's eat."

After dinner, Leonard explained to Dolores what he expected. "You will be first in command."

"I know I can handle this job," she said with confidence.

"I have no doubts. Why do you think I offered it to you?"

It was midnight when they finished. "I have to get home. Though my sitter is staying with me now, I still want to be there before my kids go to sleep. There will be a lot of work for me tomorrow."

"Don't worry. I kept you late. You deserve a few hours' sleep."

The next day, Dolores slept two hours longer and she felt invigorated. Never had she been so eager to do a job since that first day with Marshall Field. When she got to work, Leonard was waiting for her. "Hi, sweet. Follow me, please."

Dolores did as he said, not saying anything, and followed him.

"We're here." He stopped at the front of the first office.

"Nice." She sat in the cushioned chair behind the mahogany desk. Her derriere sank in the cool, thick, brown leather and she swiveled the chair around a couple of times.

"This is your office. Feel comfortable. Decorate. Make yourself at home."

She popped her fingers and yelled, "All right!"

The next few days were like a dream to Dolores. Everything was going well. She had many ideas, and began planning and inventing new ways to improve sales and productions. When she had finished her rough draft, she was about to have it typed, when Leonard entered her office.

He gazed at the papers in her hand. "What's all this?"

She handed the papers to him. "Read this and tell me what you think."

He sat on the edge of her desk and began reading. When he had finished, he looked at her for a moment.

"Ok, it's over. You don't like what you've read."

He jumped off the desk and began waving the papers in the air. "Our own designers and fashions? I tapped a gold mine when I hired you."

"Are you saying that to be nice?" She clutched her desk and held her breath. "You can tell me. I can take your thoughts."

"Sweet," he said, hugging her. "I'm going to put this to work right away."

She beamed and started telling him more. "We can have fashion shows once a month with professional makeup artist, hair stylists and a manicurist."

"Go on," he urged. I'm seeing visions of dollar signs in my head. Tell me more."

She continued, watching his face for approval. "The customers can pay a nominal fee for these services."

He picked her up and swung her around a few times. "You're savvy as well as beautiful."

Dolores' eyes gleamed, her face brightened; she was beside herself with joy. "Nobody ever praised me so highly. Those words mean a lot."

"You deserve more than words. Expect three figures on your next paycheck. Let's celebrate."

Her eyes filled with excitement, reveling in his admiration for her. She took his arm and they rode the elevator to the street. "Where are we going?"

"Let's start with lunch. Come, my lovely princess."

Herman drove them to the Benehana of Tokyo Restaurant. "Let's not go back to work. I'll take you home. You get ready for a night of fun." He gave her a big hug. "My appreciation to you."

"I can't leave the kids alone."

"Got it all taken care of. Hattie is going to stay with them."

Later that evening, Dolores was almost ready when she heard a knock on the door. Michelle opened the door and stared at Leonard. He smiled down at her. "Hello, young lady. Do you remember Hattie?"

She scrutinized Hattie before calling Dolores, "Mommy, Mr. Leonard is here with Ms. Hattie."

"Don't keep them outside. Take them to the living room, please."

Michelle did, as she was told, and then left the room. She told James that their sitter was in the living room and he peeked inside the room. Five minutes later, Dolores entered the room wearing a black, silk dress cut low to the waist, opened in back, high in front and sleeveless.

Leonard stood and went toward her, his eyes both hot and tender as he gazed at her. "You look great in that dress."

Dolores smiled, kissed her children goodnight and went along with Leonard. He took her to Trader Vic's at the Palmer House Hotel for dinner and dancing. It was three a.m. when he brought her home. "I feel guilty for keeping you out so late. I'll understand if you stay home tomorrow."

"I can't. Tomorrow is the day to contact the designers and make up artists."

"Ok, then sleep late. I'll send the car for you."

Dolores got to her office before noon. Dozens of designers and dressmakers, people whom she thought would be first rate, sat in her outer office waiting to be interviewed. It went on like this for weeks before she finally chose those whom she thought would give her dedication and hard work. "The designers and models are having a dress rehearsal this noon," she informed him, not taking her eyes from the sketches.

"Let Bob Green supervise." He took the sketches from her and laid them aside. "You need a break."

"I've got to be here." She refused to move, and took back the sketches.

"If you get sick, everything will go to pot." He pulled her out of her chair and gently guided her to the door.

She acted as If she were on roller skates, pulling back, sliding until she relented. "Ok, but let's eat at Don's Restaurant around the corner."

An hour later, Leonard and Dolores returned to her office.

Bob was waiting by the door, excited. "Mrs. Brown, everything is ready for the rehearsal."

She rushed toward him, her dark hair swinging around her shoulder. "Did the invitations arrive?"

Bob didn't say anything, just smiled and handed one of the invitations to her.

Dolores opened the gold and white envelope, removed the card and read aloud, "Velasco's Fashions And Furs present an array of spring and summer fashions. Come see the new trends in hairstyles and makeup. Door prizes awarded." She handed the invitation back to Bob. "Have one sent to every customer."

"Right away." He hurried toward the mailroom.

"You've got them hopping, sweet. I'm impressed."

Her smile broadened and satisfaction pursed her lips. "It doesn't take much. They're willing participants."

"Even so, it couldn't have been done without you."

A part of her reveled in his open admiration of her and her heart sang with delight, but she acted modest. "You're just partial, Leonard Velasco."

"I am when it comes to you, sweet." He wrapped his arms around her.

Velasco's was full with customers at noon. Dolores stepped on the makeshift stage and began the show. "Good afternoon, ladies and gentleman. Welcome to Velasco's. Our gorgeous models are waiting to show you fashions in three hem lengths: sport, casual and formal wear; including crepes, linens, silks and light weight cottons. She waved her hand, the curtains opened, the models appeared on stage, and she explained everything from formal gowns to swim wear.

27

Two hours later, after everyone had gone, she lay on Leonard's sofa, in his office, looking ethereal and unreal in the dim light from the floor lamp. "I'm pooped." She rested her head on the sofa pillars.

"I'll take you home." He helped her to her feet.

After getting out of Leonard's car, Dolores took the elevator to her apartment, opened the door and fell into bed without changing her clothes.

The next morning, on her way to work, Dolores got a New York Times newspaper and turned to the style section. "We're a hit." Later that day, she called all of the employees to her office. "I'm giving a party. Champagne and cocktails for everybody."

Leonard raised his glass to her. "I knew things would start to move once you took over. Thanks sweet."

She clinked her glass to his. "You're going to see sales like you wouldn't believe."

"Oh, I believe." He laughed and took a sip of champagne. There's no mistaking that fact."

"You've got a staff that is not afraid of hard work, loves accomplishments and gets the job done," she reminded him.

Chapter Three

After the employees had left the office, Leonard drew Dolores in his arms and took her mouth with his in a fierce kiss that revealed his hunger for her. She realized and felt the message that he was sending and she pulled away. The fire in his loins must've ached when he felt embarrassed, lowered his eyes partway, and tugged at his crotch to ease the pain. "Let's get out of here." He clicked the switch to turn off the lights.

Leonard's action toward her had unleashed a fire within her, something she was afraid of at this point in her life, but she knew that it was merely a matter of time until he would declare his intentions for her. All she had to do was to smile at him and he'd give her anything she wanted. These thoughts were against her better judgment and she tried to cool her thoughts and desires by talking about her plans, and her voice quivered. "It's going to take two years to get the other stores on track."

"You can't do it overnight," he said, still gazing at her. "Let's take a vacation."

She met the heart-rending tenderness in his eyes. "You're too much."

"I got a place in Rio De-Janeiro. Bring the children along."

"You want to take my kids?" Her heart did a funny little leap, and she had love in her eyes for him. Then she put her arms around him. They will love you for thinking of them." When she got home, she called her children to the living room. "I've got something to tell you." She watched their little ears perk up, waiting to hear what she had to say. "Mr. Velasco has invited us to his villa in Rio."

"Mommy, for real?" Michelle danced in front of her.

"You bet," she answered, throwing her head back on the sofa and laughing.

"Rio?" Michelle asked again. "Wait till my friends hear about this."

"When can we leave?" James asked.

"What about this Friday?" Dolores answered.

"Wow!" James exclaimed. "I'm packing now."

That Friday morning, Leonard sent Herman to bring Dolores and her children to the airport where they met and boarded the plane to Brazil. When they landed, Leonard rented a limousine to take them to his beautiful villa overlooking the ocean, white sand, mountains and lagoons nearby.

"Cool," Michelle said, smiling at Leonard.

"Who is game for a ride to the top of Sugar Loaf Mountain?" Leonard asked. "We can ride up to the Corcovado Mountains." He had planned some type of recreation everyday.

James and Michelle loved the outing. Leonard had charmed Michelle. "You're fun to be with, Mr. Leonard." Her eyes were shining as she smiled up at him.

"When you're having fun, I'm happy." After having fun with the children, on the beach, he left them in the water and joined Dolores. She was stretched out on a beach lounger under the sun. A large straw hat and sunglasses shaded her eyes. He sat beside her on the vacant chair. His eyes, hidden by his sunglasses, moved leisurely over her soft curvy body. Her light-blue, one-piece swimsuit was clinging to every curve. "Beautiful!" He exclaimed and shifted his sunglasses.

Dolores glanced over at him; somewhat uncomfortable because of the way he gazed at her. She nodded her head. "Yes, perfect. The weather is warm and breezy."

"I wasn't talking about the weather, but that too is to my liking."

She smiled but didn't respond, and Leonard put his sunglasses on, lied back in his lounger and pretended to watch others on the beach, but kept his eyes on her. He wanted her, needed her, and he was going to do everything in his power to have her.

Neither of them said anything for the next few minutes. Then the children came out of the water. They ran and popped sand on others lying on beach towels. Michelle flopped down next to Dolores. "Can we get lunch? I'm hungry."

Dolores swung her legs down on the sand. "Ok. I've had enough sun. What about you, Leonard?"

"I'm about as bronze as I'm going to get." He got up. I can use a drink and some nourishment."

Dolores gazed at Leonard's suntan. She was conscious of his good looks, his smooth tan skin, and high cheek-bones, a prominent nosed, framed by a thin mustache, connecting the beard on his chin and a wide smile, which always showed very white teeth. She admired his sharp profile and the way that he held his head high with pride and self-confidence. Leonard could discuss just about any subject. He was good company and she thought him to be extremely intelligent, but, at the moment, a new man wasn't what she needed in her life.

When they got back to the villa, the cook had set the table and lunch was ready. They went to shower and dress. Leonard emerged from his bedroom casually dressed in navy-blue slacks and a white sport shirt with the collar matching the slacks.

Dolores wore white Capri pants decorated with colorful beach balls and a watercolor tunic. She tied her hair in a ponytail with a floral animal print scarf.

Michelle wore red plaid Jamaican shorts and a red shirt, and James wore khaki pants and a windjammer. Leonard escorted Dolores to the table and Michelle and James followed.

They had been in Brazil for three weeks when Dolores had decided it was time to go home, interrupting their plans to spend another day. "I appreciate the fact everybody likes being here, but I want to get back to work."

"Aw, Mom, let's stay," Michelle said, pleading. "We haven't taken the boat ride to the Guanabara Bay."

"Yeah! Come on, Mom," Leonard said, in a boyish tone, holding Dolores' hand.

"No. Three weeks are long enough," she answered, sounding like the heavy.

They all made a sad face, including Leonard.

Dolores rolled her eyes toward the sky. "Leonard, help me out here."

He continued teasing her. "I don't want to go, Mom."

Dolores relented. "Ok. Three days more. After that, we're going home."

They rushed her, hugging her, and fell on the sand with them on top of her and Leonard underneath.

Three days later, they were back in New York. "Our summer fun is over," Michelle said. "We go back to school in three days."

"There's more to life than fun," Dolores reminded her. "We live, work and grow."

"Then there's fun," Michelle said and laughed.

Dolores chased her and swatted her derriere. Velasco's was her baby and she ran it like a military sergeant. Her staff worked hard, but she rewarded them when they did well, and they loved her. On her first day back to work, she found herself in the middle of decisions. "I should get started with the staff in Paris."

Leonard was pleased. "When do you want to leave?"

"The day after tomorrow." She continued chatting, absently, reading the flight schedule. "The traffic seems less hectic at the airport on that day."

"Ok. Set it up."

"Set it up? That's the easy part." What was she going to do about James? Growing up without a father had been hard and worse when his mother wasn't around.

"I know that look on your face," Leonard said. "What's troubling you?"

"It's James. I don't spend enough time with him." She folded her arms and reluctantly admitted. "He needs a man around."

Those words were what he had been waiting to hear, since he was doing everything he could to be with her children. It was part of his plan to later propose marriage. "Say no more. When should I come over?"

"I can't ask you to give up your time to be with an eight year old."

He put his hands on her shoulders, drawing her close, forcing her to look him in the eye. "I'd love to spend time with him. Nothing would please me more."

"What would I do without you?" She put her arms around him and kissed his lips softly. When she realized what she had done, she moved away from him. "I'd better get home." When she got home, she placed a call to Mama Kate. "I'm going to Paris, Mama, for business."

"Leaving them kids again?" She sounded critical. "If you got no time for them you ought to send them to me."

Dolores didn't want to argue. "Thanks, Mama, but Leonard is staying with them.

"Sounds like you done lucked up a good man."

"Besides you, Leonard is the only friend I have."

"Speaking of men, that bum is back in town."

"Sonny?" She almost strangled on her own saliva.

"Called here asking for you. I hung up on him. But not before giving him a piece of my mind."

"That's good to know. My lawyer can serve the divorce papers now." After talking with Mama Kate, she placed a call to her lawyer; thinking of how she had tried serving papers to Sonny and Virginia wouldn't tell anyone where he could be found.

Dolores' last day in New York was fabulous. Leonard gave her a bon voyage party. All of the employees were invited. Julienne and the other models realized how much Leonard cared for Dolores, and they too began to like her. They crowded around her to wish her well. "Lots of Luck," Julienne said, hugging her.

"Later that night, Leonard took Dolores to Kennedy Airport and after arriving at Orly Airport, she was met by a chauffeur in a long black Cadillac limousine.

"Bonsoir, Mademoiselle. I'm Maurice, hired by Monsieur Velasco as your personal driver."

Warmth surged through her and she said, "That man is always around when I need him."

"Wee, Mademoiselle. I'm to take you to his villa in the country."

"This is too much!" She said, thinking admirably of Leonard.

Maurice helped her into the car and drove off. After arriving at the villa, Dolores had dinner, a hot bath, and went to bed.

8 o'clock the next morning, she dressed and called Maurice to drive her to the shop, and she was outside Velasco's knocking.

Mrs. Brown, I'm Hurley." He shook her hand. "You're an early bird."

"Wasn't she the one who caught the worm?" She said in jest.

He laughed and his stomach shook like a bowl of jelly and he replied, "You got me on that one."

He must weigh all of three hundred pounds, she thought as she gazed at his protruding belly.

They went to his office and he handed her the financial ledger. When she had finished reading the balances of sales revenue and merchandise pages, she passed her plan to him. "Make a note of these proposals."

"Right away." He nodded his head. "Most of the staff here is a hard worker. It'll be clock work."

"I want a reporter from the style section of the most read newspaper for a full page advertisement." She waved her pencil in the air. "Include one from the best magazine."

In the weeks that followed, Dolores interviewed models, hairdressers and the best designers Paris had to offer. Then there were more meetings. "Fellow employees, you'll change this store's image with a new way of handling its clientele. The main focus line is on fashions and emphasis on selling." Again Dolores had handled the meetings like a military sergeant. The employees took to her, and that made her job easier, but it had taken six months longer than she had expected.

One morning, after Dolores had gotten to work, an old gentleman came into the shop. "Ezcusez-moi, Mademoiselle. I'd like to order a fur."

She turned and gazed at a svelte man with long, salt and pepper hair and a gray mustache. The rest of his face was clean-shaven, and he had small, dark brown eyes that seem to stare into her soul when he looked at her. She forced a smile and asked, "Any particular style and size?"

"My wife is stately," He answered, scrutinizing her.

"I'll model a few coats and we can order her size." She moved to the rack of furs, slipping into one and slowly walking in front of him.

His eyes followed her every movement. Then he beckoned to her to come to him. When she went over to him, he lifted the hem of the coat, rubbed his hand back and forth over the pelts and felt the arms in the same manner, his eyes still fixed on her.

She had modeled several coats before he had chosen one. "I'll take the Ranch Mink. Bring it to my home."

"The store will have it delivered, sir. Give your address to the sale's clerk."

"I want you to show it to my wife," he insisted.

"That could be arranged." She thought if the old goat were rich, it wouldn't do to hurt Leonard's business. She took his name and address, and placed it in the store's file.

The next day, before noon, Dolores called Maurice to drive her to Jacques' Glauert's chateau. When she arrived, his butler let her enter and led her to the drawing room. Twenty minutes later, a dark haired, beautiful woman, who appeared to be sixty years old, entered the room. "Let me see the coat," she said, in a high tone manner, with no mention of who she was.

Dolores, assuming that she was Mrs. Glauert, took the coat out of the garment bag and held it up in front of her. The woman ran her fingers through the fur.

"Put it on. I want to see how it fits."

Dolores got into the coat and walked back and forth in front of her.

"Let me have the coat." She took the coat and slipped it over her round protruding, pudgy body. She walked around, did a few turns, smiled and without saying a word, walked out of the room.

"Ill -mannered witch!" Dolores muttered.

Mr. Glauert entered carrying his checkbook. "My wife is pleased. What's the price?"

"Twenty-five thousand."

He wrote the check and handed it to her, then went over to the coffee table and got a white envelope. He handed it to her. Dolores opened the envelope and glanced at two hundred dollars. "Thank you, sir." She hurried out to the limousine.

At the end of the day, Dolores went home, ate dinner and took a hot bubble bath. She settled back in the tub, closed her eyes, and tried to forget the office. She thought about Leonard. Then the phone rang and she answered to hear a deep baritone voice.

"I'm sending a car for you tonight."

"You have the wrong number, sir. She was about to hang up and he quickly spoke.

"Mademoiselle, Brown, have you read my invitation?"

She got out of the tub, fished in her purse and found a smooth white note, engraved in black embossed letters. She went back to the phone. "Thanks for the invite, but I must decline."

"Nonsense. Come and have fun. You'll be my son's guest."

She became annoyed and tried not to lose her cool. "I don't go to parties alone."

He continued, "I'll come and escort you. Don't be difficult."

"No thank you. I must hang up now. Bye." Dolores got back in the tub and stayed thirty minutes. When she was dressing for bed, the doorbell rang. She answered. "How impudent!" She said, in Mr. Glauert's face. "What do you not understand about the word, no?"

"Please, Mademoiselle. I'm one of Monsieur Velasco's friends and best customer. Do me the honor of accepting my invitation."

She thought for a moment. The old goat did buy an expensive coat today, and she didn't want to ruin it for Leonard. "Wait in the car till I'm ready." She went through her closet twice, before she chose a gown that Leonard had admired. It was black and silver sequined, slightly low cut in front, not too revealing, and with t-straps. She slipped into the dress, selected silver shoes and hurried outside.

He opened the door to his black Mercedes Limousine and helped her inside. "Glad you changed your mind."

"What choice did you give me?" she said and sat beside him.

"I presented an offer you couldn't refuse," he answered with an air of self-righteous dignity.

Dolores didn't say anything, just rolled her eyes at him and sat quietly while he talked about his son. "Philip is single, handsome and a good catch for the right woman."

Probably a boor," she mumbled under her breath.

"Did you say something?

No." She shook her head and smiled.

They arrived at his chateau. He got out and escorted her inside and introduced her to a few guest. "These people don't matter. I want you to meet my son." He took her hand and waded through crowd of people who tried to chat with him as he passed them. He found his son in another room. "Philip, this is the beautiful woman from Velasco's."

Philip smiled, brought her hand to his lips and kissed it lightly. "Father, she's not only beautiful, you forgot to add goddess."

Dolores smiled and whispered, through her teeth, "Just like his father; full of shit." She gazed at him. He looked like him, only shorter, with a beard and not quite as heavy. His hair was darker. He had the same cleft in his chin and his dark eyes twinkled when he smiled.

Still holding her hand, he suddenly pulled her to into his arms. "Let's dance." He guided her to the room where everyone was dancing and began a rhumba.

Dolores tried keeping in step until she added a few extra steps of her own. Everyone stopped dancing to watch them.

"You're good," he said, stepping to the beat.

She began enjoying dancing and found herself laughing at everything Philip said. They continued to dance as the orchestra played several tunes. "Aren't you neglecting your guest?"

"No. They're happy when I'm happy. Look around. See any sad faces?"

"They seem happy."

"Sure. Don't worry." He twirled her around on the floor several more times before the music stopped, and danced again until the party had ended. It was 2 o'clock in the morning. Everyone, except a few guests, went home. Dolores got her purse and headed for the door.

Philip stopped her. "Stay the night."

"I can't. I have a reputation to uphold."

"This is 'Gay Paree.'" He purred the name. "No one thinks of reputation. Come have some wine. Dance."

"I'll stay," she said against her better judgment. "No more wine, though."

"Ok. I'll drink. You listen." He reached for a bottle of wine. He drank and boasted about his escapades with women.

Dolores grew sleepy and wanted to go to her room. Reluctantly, he showed her to one of the guest rooms, and wobbled back to the party room.

11 o'clock the next morning, the maid was opening the draperies in Dolores' room. She stirred, opened her eyes slowly and glanced at her watch.

The maid gazed at her over her eyeglasses. "Morning, Madame. Mr. Glauert has selected these clothes for you."

Dolores glanced at the riding attire, on the chair, next to her bed, and she hopped out, showered and dressed in her own clothes. She hurried down the hall and bumped into Philip. "You're in time for breakfast." He held her hand.

She shook her head. "No thanks. I've got to leave."

"Not before you eat." He pulled her into the dining room. "Sit!" He went around the table and sat across from her. He winked at her and said, "You're as beautiful in the morning as the night before."

The other guest at the table stared at her, then at him and smiled.

Dolores' face turned red and she began filling her plate with sausages and miniature sweet bread.

We're playing polo after breakfast," Philip announced. "Why aren't you dressed in the riding attire?"

"I don't play." She hated admitting her shortcomings.

"No problem," he said and smiled arrogantly. "I'm a good teacher."

"Thanks, but I've got to get home. Maybe, some other time?"

Mr. Glauert moved a seat over and sat beside her. "It's Saturday. Enjoy your day."

Dolores laughed and said, "You Glauerts are impossible. She excused herself and went back to her room to change into the riding attire.

"I've selected a tame horse for you, and a spirited one for me." He helped her mount, and then led her onto their private field. "Let the game begin." He announced.

Dolores followed him and tried to swing her mallet, but she lost to a guest who rode behind her and struck the ball, sending it through the goalpost.

Philip yelled and made a victory sign with his fingers.

An hour later, Dolores got dressed and Philip called his chauffeur to drive her home.

The next morning, when Dolores had arrived at the store, Mr. Hurley was puffing and running after her. "We're ready for the noon show."

"Right on, Mr. Hurley." She walked swiftly to her office, not bothering to slow down for him.

"Got to keep the ball rolling." He rushed away, wiping sweat from his face.

During the showing, Philip, took a seat down front and ordered a dress. He sent the dress with a note to Dolores' office. "Wear the dress and have dinner with me."

After the store had closed, Dolores rushed home to shower and was dressed by the time Philip came to get her. They went to Le Grande Vefour,

17 Rue de Beaujolais. Philip ordered from the menu for them. "Entrecote bordelaise, de la biere, haricots verts, torte Chantilly y café au laite."

Impressed, Dolores asked, "What did you order?"

"Rib steak prepared with red Bordeaux, garnished with onions, garlic and mushrooms, Beer pie with whipped cream and coffee," he answered and kissed her hand.

"Too much. I can't eat it all."

"You should eat more. Don't worry about fat."

"Forget you," she said and laughed.

They continued to laugh and enjoy themselves, and after they had finished dinner, Philip drove her home and asked to come inside for a drink. They sat on the sofa listening to music when suddenly; Philip took her in his arms. "Let me buy a chateau in the country for you."

Dolores was startled. "Why?" She asked, examining his motives.

"I want a mistress __a desirable woman like you who'd be there for me."

Dolores got angry. "You've got the wrong woman. I'll never be kept by any man." She got up and hurried to her front door. "Get out!"

He grinned and declared, "We're going to be together. Think it over and let me know."

"Don't count on it, honey," she said, in a hard voice. "You see, Philip, you don't turn me on."

"Oh, you'll call me, baby. Once you and I make love, you'll be mine completely."

"Go home, inhale and wait for my call."

Dolores' time in Paris was ending. She was pleased with the accomplishments at the store and the customers were happy. Before leaving, she called a last minute meeting with the employees. "I want to thank all of you for helping me to make Velasco's a success." Their hugs made her feel that they were genuinely sorry to see her go.

"You made us feel like family." Mr. Hurley said, wiping his eyes. "I'm a big baby."

Dolores laughed and hugged him.

When Dolores' plane landed in New York, Leonard and her children were waiting. "I received the reviews. You're terrific!"

"You're pretty terrific, too. My kids look healthy." She laughed and poked James' stomach. James giggled and hugged her.

"It's good having you home, Mommy, Michelle said. "I missed you."

"I missed all of you, too. Come here." She put her arms around them in a circle.

Herman drove them home, and Leonard stayed to have dinner with them. After Leonard left, Dolores took a shower, changed into something comfortable and was about to get into bed, with a good book, when Leonard phoned.

"You've generated a lot of wealth for me."

"I'm happy you gave me the job, and a chance to prove myself."

"You're getting an increase in pay, young lady. How does a hundred thousand a year sound?"

Though she was thrilled, she couldn't speak. She had carved a niche for herself, second in command, and in charge of her life.

When she didn't answer, Leonard thought that she was displeased. "Ok. Name your price."

"No." She said finally. "It's more than I expected." When she and Leonard had finished talking, she called her children. "Want to go house hunting this weekend?"

"Mommy, you mean it?" Michelle asked, doing her usual dance. James pounced on the bed and kissed Dolores.

"I got a raise!" She said and joined Michelle dancing

Saturday morning, Dolores and her children met the realtor and before the day was over, he'd shown them six houses. One house was in Terry Town. They decided, unanimously, on an eighteen room, ranch—style, and a couple of blocks from Leonard's home. "Moving day will be two weeks from today," Dolores declared.

"I love this house," James said. But I'll miss the park."

"We will return to the park," Dolores promised. "I love the park, too."

Dolores and her children went home and began to pack. Leonard came over to help. While he moved boxes and furniture, he talked about the business. "You've done well. Now I have a proposition for you."

"What's on your mind?"

"I purchased another store while you were in Paris. The retail-shopping district in Manhattan near 34th Street."

"Smart move." She threw her thumbs up.

"It's a partnership, but you will have full control coordinating everything."

"Is this ok with the partner?

"I told him about you and he has agreed. You can take over after you've settled in your new home."

She thought about the new shop and wondered what Leonard's partner was like, and she couldn't wait to get to work the next morning. Leonard had sent several invitations to customers announcing the new shop. Around 10 o'clock, Dolores handled the first showing of furs. Leonard came to the shop at noon with a few buyers and wanted to have lunch. She was invited.

Herman drove them to the Roosevelt on 45th Street and Madison Avenue. They were seated and were soon joined by Leonard's partner. "Everyone, meet my new partner, Philip Glauert."

Dolores almost choked on her food.

"Philip is the son of an old friend."

Throughout the evening, whenever Leonard asked anything, Philip would ask Dolores for her opinion.

After dinner, Leonard made a suggestion, "What say you to dancing for the rest of the evening?"

"Sounds great to me," Dolores said.

Everyone agreed, and they left and went to the Hotel's Persian Room. After being seated, Philip rushed to ask Dolores for a dance.

"No thanks," she flatly said, trying to disguise her annoyance in front of the others.

"Go head. Enjoy yourself," Leonard said.

Dolores gritted her teeth and gave Philip a brutal and unfriendly stare as he took her hand and led her to the dance floor.

"You fit snugly in my arms." He held her tighter, lifted her chin and forced her to look into his eyes. "I can do a lot for you."

She gave him a push and put a distance between them, smiled pleasantly, took in a deep breath and informed him, "No more than I can do for myself."

"You'll change your mind." He smiled, sardonically, and danced her around the floor.

"I can't take much more of this." She let go of him and returned to her seat.

"Tired?" Leonard asked, suspecting nothing.

She shook her head, "Yes."

"Come. I'll take you home."

When Herman stopped the car in front of her apartment, Leonard saw her to her door. "Get some rest, sweet."

It was moving day. Dolores followed the moving van till it stopped in front of her new home. James and Michelle got out of the car and ran inside. "I'm taking the blue room," declared James.

"I want the room with the view to the back yard," Michelle said.

Dolores took the master bedroom facing the street. After they had gotten everything in place, with the help of the movers, Dolores prepared dinner, and they enjoyed having the first meal in their new home.

The next morning, after a good night's sleep, in quiet surroundings, minus horns blowing, the sound of elevator doors opening and people playing music, Dolores felt wonderfully relaxed. She arrived at the shop early to prepare her schedule for the week's line merchandise and fashion show.

Chapter Four

It was 2 o'clock p.m. when several out of town buyers entered the shop. Dolores, along with the other models, showed several furs until 8 o'clock that night, and at closing time, the last buyer was getting his purchases wrapped.

When Dolores got home, the phone was ringing. "Why don't someone answer the phone? Michelle, James, where are you?" She ran and picked up the phone. "Mama Kate? What's wrong?"

"I fell on the front porch. Broke my leg. These old bones ain't hard as they once were."

"The kids and I will be there. Don't worry." When she finished talking, she called Leonard.

"Want me to come with you, sweet?"

"No. Stay with the business. We won't stay long."

Four and a half hours later, Dolores and the children stepped off the plane at the Oakland Airport, rented a car and drove to Mama Kate's house. She was seated on a chase lounge in her bedroom.

"Look at my babies!" She held her arms out to them. "You done a great job of raising them."

"I just have good kids," she said, realizing how blessed that she was, as a single parent, and grateful for the precious moments she had spent teaching them. She gazed at Michelle, thinking how beautiful she was with her long, black hair braided and covered with colorful beads. Her smooth caramel skin, prominent nose, and big brown eyes, made her strikingly more like her than James. He was more like Sonny, but had honey colored skin, straight, black hair and a pug shaped nose. Thank God, he didn't have Sonny's manner. James was quiet, calm, and knew what he wanted out of life.

Dolores got settled, fixed dinner and talked about New York. "You ought to come home with me Mama, You'd enjoy the restaurants, shopping centers and stores."

"I enjoy it right here," she said and laughed. "You ought to take the children to the mall on Airport Boulevard. Buy them something nice."

"I'll do that tomorrow, but now, I'm going to get some sleep."

Later that night, after everyone was asleep, the phone rang. Dolores answered, sleepily, "Jones's residents."

"Hi, babe. Heard you were coming home."

The sound of that familiar voice woke her, and she opened her eyes wide. "What do you want, Sonny?"

"I want to see my kids."

"Oh, so now they're your kids? You gave them up when you got into drugs."

"Come on, don't disc me. I've changed."

"Changed? You?" She exhaled and laughed.

"Yeah! I sell cars now. Got my own dealership. I want to get to know my kids."

"It's too late."

He stopped acting smart and started pleading, "Please, let me see them."

Begging, she thought. The Sonny she knew never begged.

"Let me come over tomorrow," he continued, in a low tormented voice.

"I'll think about it and let you know." She hung up without saying good-bye.

That morning, Dolores sat quietly at breakfast, thinking of Sonny's request. She got out of her chair and paced back and forth.

"What's wrong?"

"Sonny wants to see the kids."

"You don't owe that fool nothing. Don't let him near them."

"You're right. He can forget it."

That evening, they were looking at television when the doorbell rang. Michelle answered the door.

"My little girl," Sonny said, grinning at her.

"Mommy, there's a man at the door." She gazed up at him with her nose turned up.

Dolores ran to the door. "You got to be sick," she yelled in is face. "Thinking you can come here_ expecting things to be all right_ after what you did?"

He reached out and grasped her hand. "Help me."

"Oh, for Christ sake," she said, jerking her hand free.

Michelle and James stood there looking at him and Dolores relented. "Come on in."

Sonny went toward them with his arms out to hug them. Michelle and James stood motionless. Sonny hugged Michelle and looked at James standing behind his sister. 'Who's that standing behind you? I bet his name is James."

James didn't move. Nor did he say anything.

Sonny sighed heavily, his voice was filled with anguish. "I'm your daddy."

Dolores interrupted, "Where have you been all this time?"

"Pennsylvania. I worked the coal mines."

"Why didn't you send money to your kids?" She stared at him with haughty rebuke.

"Didn't have none to send. I got lucky at cars and came back here."

"All these years you've been gone ---was it worth it?"

"Got money now," he jingled his pockets. "Came back for you and the kids."

Her accusing voice stabbed the air and she shook with impotent rage. "After what you did to me?"

"C'mon, babe, you know I didn't mean to hurt you." He crooned in his usual voice, whenever he tried to persuade her.

"Hurt? It was sheer hell." She sliced the air with her hands, stopping short of hitting him. "I had no husband. The kids, no father."

"Go 'head. Slap me if it'd make you feel better. I deserve it." He braced himself for a slap, realizing that his sexy manner no longer worked.

Mama Kate interrupted, "It's time for dinner and we don't have extras."

"I can take a hint. I'm leaving, but I'm begging you. Let me come back to see my kids."

The long deep look they exchanged infuriated Dolores, but she relented for the children's sake.

After that night, Sonny came everyday for two weeks until Dolores and the children returned to New York. Dolores tried to forget her encounter with Sonny by working harder at the shop. She didn't take time to prepare breakfast, leaving earlier than usual to get to work, and waiting until noon for snacks, and then going to a restaurant for dinner. This particular evening, she had decided to go to K-Paul's New York. It was crowded, but she managed to be seated when everyone else was seated. She ordered a Cajun martini, while waiting for an order of blackened tuna, and read her newspaper. Suddenly, she became aware of someone standing beside her.

"Mind if I share your table?"

Dolores gazed up into the largest pair of gray eyes she had ever seen. He must be a wide receiver, she thought, because his muscles are doing injury to that elegant brown silk suit. The way he stood told her that he was doing well for himself. Her heart began to pound. She was completely taken by him and that scared her. Get a grip, girl, she told herself, you know how you are in choosing the wrong man.

"May I?" he asked again, his boldly handsome face smiling warmly down at her.

"Sure! Why not?" Why did she say that? She immediately scolded herself. This was a stranger, and she should be wary of strange men, especially ones who looked as sexy as him. But there was something about him that made her feel at ease.

He sat and began reading the menu. Dolores continued to read and to steal a look at him. He commented on an article from the page of her paper that was facing him.

"More killings. We need gun control."

"You're right." She lowered the paper and faced him.

"I'm Blake Edwards." He extended his hand. "I don't usually stop to eat dinner, before going home, but this evening, I'm starved."

"I know just what you mean, but I didn't anticipate this crowd."

"Is it always this crowded?"

"My first time here."

The waitress came with her food. He stared at it and ordered the same. He soon had his food and they talked as they ate. "I own a business selling financial products: certificate of deposits, bonds and other investments."

"I'm in the fashion and fur business."

"The way you look makes that easy to believe."

"Thanks," she said, and turned her head a little to prevent him seeing her blush.

They talked a few minutes more and then she glanced at her watch. "It's late. Got to get back to the store." She got up to leave.

"Wait! What's your name?"

"Dolores Brown," she answered, reluctantly.

"It was great sharing your table, Dolores. What about dinner tomorrow?"

"Can't. I have a date with my fashion designers."

"Lunch? What's your phone number?"

"Give yours to me. I'll phone you," she said, half smiling.

He handed her his business card and she pretended to put it in her purse, but threw it in the trash when she got to her car.

Dolores was spending long hours at the stores. The designers and dressmakers were working almost around the clock, and she was in the center of it, driving them, commanding them to finish with the entire array of fashions in three months.

One evening, when she was in a rush, she stopped at K-Paul's for a sandwich. Blake came in and sat beside her. "By the way, I have a new phone number. Is that why I never heard from you?"

Dolores laughed and stared at him, and he studied her face and knew that she hadn't called. "Why?" he asked, yearning for a plausible explanation.

"I didn't want to be an easy pickup. I learned long ago, that's trouble."

He agreed, "That's understandable. What about dinner tonight?"

What a nudge, she thought. Better put a stop to him now. "No," she said, in a confident even—tempered voice, thinking it would deter him.

His face took on a look like that of a little boy, who had asked for a toy and hadn't received what he had wanted. He leaned over and whispered to her. "You know me now. Please have dinner with me."

His persistence amused her. Such style and determination warranted admiration. "Ok." She gave him her personal card.

That night, when she closed the shop, Blake was parked outside. He phoned her from his car, and she came out and got into his Lincoln town car. His chauffeur drove them to Maxim's Restaurant on Madison Avenue near 61st and 62nd. "You'll love the Art Nouveau décor," he said. "It reminds me of its namesake in Paris."

Paris? Oh, no, not again. Hope he isn't like those Glauert's.

When they entered the restaurant, she was pleased. "I see what you mean. This place is fabulous!"

They dined and danced most of the evening.

"This is one of the few places where you eat and dance," he said.

It was 3 o'clock a.m. when Blake took Dolores home. "Thanks for taking me to Maxim's. It was fun." She turned her head when she thought he was about to kiss her on the lips.

His breath had quickened when he inhaled her scent of wisteria flowers mingled with her clean womanly scent. He brushed her cheek with his hand. "I'll drive you to work tomorrow."

"That's not necessary."

"Will you permit me to call?"

"She called to him before entering the door, 555-6757."

It was 7 o'clock in the morning when Blake phoned Dolores from his car. He waited until she came out and his chauffeur drove them to Maxim's for breakfast. Dolores yawned through breakfast.

"Excuse me," she said. "Late night."

"I feel awful after keeping you out late." He leaned his shoulder against the seat near her.

"Don't. I loved being out with you. I'm sleepy, but I feel great."

"In that case, let's have lunch today. He rested his chin on his hand and he had a bemused smile on his face.

"The models are having a dress rehearsal. I've got to be there."

"Blake lifted his brow. "Are you kicking me to the curb?"

Dolores laughed, draped her purse across her shoulder, and answered, "I'm always on the job. With me, business comes first."

"Ok, Miss business lady, but after everything's over, you're mine."

They finished eating and his chauffeur drove her to work. When she entered the shop, Bob ran toward her. Mrs. Brown, everything is ready."

"You're the best stage manager in this city." She shook his hand and hurried to her office.

It was 2 o'clock when Dolores stepped on the temporary stage erected in the middle of the store. "Good evening, ladies and gentlemen. Welcome to Velasco's. Our beautiful models are going to show fashions in sport and casual wear."

"Everyone applauded and Dolores continued. "Our professional makeup artist has something for every skin type, and dazzling new trends in hairstyles. Sit back, relax, and enjoy."

Two hours later, after the customers had gone, Dolores went outside where Blake was waiting for her. He let her out at her door. Blake kissed her lightly on the lips and said, "I'll pick you up early tomorrow."

How early? I like to sleep late. It's my Saturday off."

"Early, early. It's a surprise."

"I don't like surprises."

"You'll like this one."

6 o'clock the next morning, Blake was knocking on Dolores' door. Barely opening her eyes, she stumbled to the door and looked through the peephole. "Blake?" She opened the door.

"Are you ready?"

"Give me a couple of minutes." She went to her bedroom and in more than an hour, she came out dressed in a white suite and white leather pumps. She hadn't taken any notice of Blake wearing jeans, a blue sports jacket and boating shoes.

"You'll have to change your clothes and don't forget your swimsuit."

Her smile quickly faded. "You have got to be kidding. It took some time for me to look like this."

"I know, and you look gorgeous, but remember, it's your surprise."

She rolled her eyes and asked, "Where is my common sense? I'm excited by, drooling over a surprise." Minutes later, she returned wearing blue slacks, a white top and tennis shoes. "This had better be good."

"Don't fret, love, you'll be happy later." He took her arm in his and led her to his car.

Dolores looked around. "Where is the surprise?"

"Not yet." He motioned to his chauffeur to drive away. They rode to Long Island and ended up at Barrier beach. "Close your eyes," he commanded.

"What for?"

"Your surprise. He put his hand over her eyes, helped her out of the car, and walked arm and arm across the sand to the water's edge, where a speed boat was waiting a few feet away. "Remove your shoes, but keep your eyes closed."

She became concerned. "I don't want to play any longer."

"Please, Dolores, just a few minutes more. Trust me."

She played along, kept her eyes closed and removed her shoes.

He led her into the water and she screamed when the cold water covered her feet.

"It's not dangerous. The water is nineteen inches deep."

"But it's cold," she said shivering. Every instinct warned her against this folly.

He helped her into the speedboat, and motioned for the captain to shove off.

"I'm going to give you a few minutes to present me with something," she said, in a firm voice. "Then, I'm going to swim ashore." The boat stopped and she heard a noise. "What's that? Sounds like metal hitting the side of the boat."

"Open your eyes."

"It's a yacht!" She ran up the gangplank and explored every room, starting with four beautifully furnished bedrooms, a game room with a bar and another room for entertaining guest. "It's breath taking."

"There's more," he said and laughed.

"I feel like a little girl shopping in a candy store. What else is there?"

"In due time." He took her arm. "Let's dance." He flipped a switch near the bar and Anthony Hamilton started singing, "Giving You the Best of Me." He was holding her tightly and she felt the beat of his heart against her own. Her head began spinning, and she felt weak. "Hold it!" she said, pushing him away to give her space.

His expression stilled and grew serious. "What's wrong?"

"I can't breathe." She pulled away and took a seat at the bar.

He stood behind her and kissed her neck, her ear, and then lifted her off the stool. He kissed her long and hard, and she wiggled out of his arms and walked away. "This is getting out of hand."

"Sorry. It was just a kiss. I didn't mean to come on so strong."

"I want to go ashore." She went toward the door.

He held her arm to stop her. "It's too late. We're sailing to the Bahamas."

A look of indignation crossed her face and she shouted, "Why didn't you tell me?"

"It's your surprise. Please, I'll be good. I won't do anything you won't like."

His sexy look made her feel more cautious. "Depends on what you mean by, nothing I wouldn't like."

"You're so suspicious." He backed away with his hands in the air.

Her voice softened a little as she tried to control her emotions. Had he overwhelmed her? "I don't have clothes, and I have to work Monday."

"Relax! Your boss knows everything. I called him. Your clothes are on board."

"What about my kids?"

"Your boss is taking care of them."

"I don't know whether to be angry or happy." She looked at him side-ways.

"Happy," he said. "We're going to have fun."

They had sailed for three hours. Blake taught her to play stud poker and black jack. They shot pool and danced. Dolores began to laugh and to feel at ease. "I have to say one thing. You know how to have fun and you know how to treat a lady."

"That's not hard when the lady is you," he said and squeezed her.

It was 4 o'clock a.m. when they went to their separate rooms, and later that morning, an hour before docking in Nassau, the cook prepared breakfast. When they finished eating, a chauffeur came aboard. "The limo awaits, my lady," Blake said, bowing in jester like an English Nobleman.

"You've got class, Blake. I like your style." She followed him down the gangplank to the car.

The chauffeur stopped in front of a white Spanish villa trimmed in brown with a brown slate roof.

They got out and went through the dark oak front door, which was surrounded by lavender nasturtiums. "Fabulous," she said, and sat in the carved wooden chair on the porch, which stretched the length of the villa.

"I'm happy you like the place. Come with me." He took her hand and pulled her out of the chair. "I'll show you to your room."

Dolores fingered the headboard. I've never slept in a wicker bed."

He motioned for her to follow him and he stood near the entrance to the bathroom. She went inside and stood over the bathtub. "I love Emerald green. It correlates well with the green tile floor. "I'd love to soak in the tub for twenty minutes."

"Later, darling, let's test the water in the pool." He opened the wicker dresser drawer and pointed to several swimwear.

"You do this often, don't you?" She stared at him out of the corner of her eye.

He smiled, hung his head and said, "I'll meet you at the pool."

Dolores chose her size and favorite color, out of several small suits, undressed and slipped into the a blue, two-piece style. She came out, took a running leap and dove into the red bottom, heart shaped pool.

Blake dove in and came to the surface beside her. They swam for an hour before he took her to town. They had lunch at Cable Beach.

"Delicious food, mellow wine and this atmosphere are relaxing." She waved her hand in the air. "Perfect."

"I knew you would like it here." He watched her enjoying the lobster tails. "After lunch, we'll play tennis and go horseback riding."

"Tennis, I can handle. Horses, no."

"It'll be fun," he insisted.

They went back to the villa and played tennis on his private court. She won two games. "You've beaten me," he said. "Let's see who will be the winner of a good horse race." He led her to the stables. "This is a tame horse." He chose one for himself. "This horse has fire in his blood." They started out, and he had gone a couple of yards before he realized that she was not beside him. He rode back to her. "Why didn't you follow me?"

She stiffened, momentarily, and after pulling the reins several times, she admitted, "This darn horse wouldn't move."

Blake laughed hard for a minute, and she got angry.

Ok, you've had your little fun. Help me off this beast."

He stopped laughing and took the reins. "Come, I'm going to teach you how to ride." He guided her horse along side his and they rode along smoothly until something spooked her horse. Her horse bolted and she fell to the ground. Before she could catch her breath he was beside her. "Sorry, darling. I should not have insisted that you ride." He took her in his arms and put her on his horse. They rode back to the villa, and after resting an hour; they dressed in their swimsuits and swam in the pool. Blake began teasing Dolores. He held her ankle preventing her from swimming. Then, he pulled her close, held her tightly in his arms and kissed her.

Her knees buckled and she felt an unwelcoming surge of excitement. Am I floating? She asked herself. Before she knew what had happened, Blake had untied her top. She held onto her top with both hands, glared at him and said, "I'm not ready to be intimate with you."

He lifted her and sat her on the edge of the pool, then hopped upon the edge beside her. "You're driving me wild! It's hard, in more ways than one.

"You promised to keep your distance."

"Oh, alright." He tied her top.

They sat and talked until he thought of something for them to do. "Let's go to town, have dinner and go dancing."

"Good," she agreed. "Dancing will keep us out of trouble."

"Want to bet?" he said, drawing in his lips and helping her up from the pool's edge.

Masterful persuasion seems to be his style, she thought with fearful clarity. Could she resist his bundle of sexy energy when she was fighting her own battle of sexual restraint? She went to her room to dress.

An hour later, Blake knocked on her door. "Hurry up, slowpoke. I'll wait by the porch."

She came out five minutes later, and Blake helped her into the car, dancing part of the rhumba. The chauffeur drove them to the yacht in the harbor, and they were taken to Paradise Island. It was 4 o'clock a.m. When they returned. Dolores was going to her room when Blake stepped in front of her and kissed her so hard that she could feel his teeth. "Marry me," he said, holding her.

I'm fond of you, Blake, but I have to be in love when I marry." Her mind was saying one thing, her heart another, and she was enjoying his persistence.

"I'm going to have you," he whispered, in her ear with his cheek pressed to hers.

"I had a man like you once," she said, pushing him aside. "He didn't have your class and money, but he was a smooth talker."

"Aw, come on. I'm serious."

"I am too," she said with a sly grin, walking backward into her room and closing her door.

Later that morning, Dolores sat at the dining table waiting for the cook to serve breakfast.

Blake entered, carrying a small gift and handed it to her. "Open it and say yes."

She opened the box and the diamond sparkled in the light of the chandelier hanging over the dining table. "I thought you understood." She handed the ring back to him.

"I know. You have to be in love. Keep it till you change your mind." He put the ring in her hand. "I won't expect anything till you're ready."

"This may never happen." She set the ring on the table. "I'm happy being single."

For the next few days, Blake did everything to show another side of him. He was attentive, respectively so, making sure not to rush her into anything, and Dolores loved every minute of it. Then, It was time to return home. "It's hard to believe two weeks have passed," she said.

"We don't have to leave."

"Yeah sure! I have a job, kids and responsibilities."

When the yacht docked in New York, they were taken ashore and Blake's chauffeur met them. He drove Dolores home. Blake kissed her lightly on the lips, trying not to overpower her with his affections. "Think of me, darling."

When Dolores got inside of her house, she thought of Blake. He's too much like Sonny and she promised herself never to get involved with a man like him. Sonny's face and the sound of his voice wouldn't leave her memory, and she felt a throbbing headache developing. She rubbed her temples until she felt sleepy.

The next morning, Leonard brought her children home. "I'm sorry about your vacation, but we can still have one." She said.

"I'm hanging with my friends for the summer," Michelle said.

"Same here, Mom," James said. "My friend, Chico, has invited me to his summer home in Monterey."

"That settles that. What can I do for you, Leonard?"

"I'd like to go over some papers."

"OK. I'll prepare dinner tonight for two. 6 o'clock?"

Chapter Five

Dolores waltzed around her kitchen, humming and clinking pots. Why was she so excited? This wasn't a date. It's business. She just wanted to make everything nice for a great boss who happened to be a special friend. Leonard arrived an hour early. Dolores opened the door, and he stood there gazing at her. "Are you having dinner in the hall, or are you coming inside?"

"I couldn't help myself," he said. "You look enchanting."

"She smiled and led him to the living room. "Have a seat. Enjoy some cool wine." She poured a glass and handed it to him.

His eyes followed her when she moved fluidly across the room. "My love, let me be your slave, give you anything you want," he mumbled under his breath so that she couldn't hear him.

She came to the room and sat beside him. "The food is almost ready."

"Good. We've a lot to accomplish tonight and I'll try not to bore you."

"Leonard?" She gazed into his eyes. "I'm never bored when I'm with you."

"We will finish what we can and I'll get out of here."

"Something is bothering you. What's wrong?"

"What could be wrong?" He turned away. "I'm rich, happy and __how was your cruise?"

"I had loads of fun. Blake loves a good time."

"Have you known him long?"

"Three months. We are friends. Nothing more."

A slow grin came across his bewildered face. "Let's finish these proposals after dinner. I'm starving."

They sat at the table and he gazed at the way she had arranged the centerpiece of white and pink roses surrounding a small waterfall in a wide mouth vase. I like your table. The colors compliments the white linen tablecloth, Pink napkins and white gold rimmed china."

"I know you love things that are different, and I prepared everything for you."

His smile became a full-out grin, and he started serving himself and tasted the veal. "Hmm, I'm having two servings of everything."

They talked about Velasco's between chewing and drinking wine. When they had finished eating, Leonard spread the papers on the table. "How soon can you start on the shops in D. C.?" He reached for the coffee.

"I'll get it," she said, and put her hand over his. He gazed at her in a way that caused her body to undulate with a sensual awareness she had never felt before.

He took the cup from her and he seemed a bit nervous. She lowered her eyes and said, "The second Thursday of this month would be the perfect time for me to go to Washington."

"How do you feel about me?" he asked, as if he had not heard a word she had said.

She was caught off guard, and quickly raised her eyes, blinked and opened her mouth to speak, "I __ you."

"Never mind," he said, his face turning red.

She took a deep breath to steady her voice and said, "You are my best friend." She put her arms around him. "I wouldn't know what to do without you."

"Friend? Is that how you see me? Ok. I've taken enough of your time." He got up. "Thanks for dinner and your help."

"Part of the process," she said. "I accepted the job, and I like working with you."

He stared at her with a doubtful expression and asked, "Want me to take you to the airport, or is what's his name taking you?"

"You're incredible, you know? Why would I want anyone but you to take me?"

He gazed at her happily, as if all of his fears had been expelled. They walked outside to his car.

"See you tomorrow." She waved, then went back inside and chuckled when she thought of the way he had acted all evening. He was jealous, the darling man, and pretty wonderful. The way he handled her kid, the things he said and did, and the values that made him who he was, made him special to her. There seemed to be nothing he didn't understand when she had a problem, or wasn't willing to help her. Then to top it all he was cute, intelligent, and fairly handsome.

The phone rang, when she was preparing for bed.

"Hi darling. Ready to become Mrs. Edwards?"

"Blake! Where are you?"

"New Delhi. What about my question?"

"Come home. Let's talk about your question."

"I'll be there for as long as it takes to take off and land."

They talked for two hours before she hung up the phone and she lay in bed thinking of what it would be like married to Blake. Life would never be dull, there would be many parties, she would be treated like a queen of her domain and she could expect a lot of loving. What more could any woman ask for out of life?"

Dolores got to work early that morning, but instead of tackling her usual workload, her thoughts were of Blake and when he was coming home. She would plan a delicious dinner with Chicken Cardoon Bleu, rice, green beans with almonds and sweet potato pie. Candlelight would be better with red roses, white linens and her rosewood china.

When work had ended, she rushed home and began preparing the meal. Everything was ready by 5:30. 6 o'clock came and went, then 8 o'clock. Blake hadn't called. Then the phone rang and she ran to answer. "Blake _____I."

"Hi, sweet. May I take you to dinner tonight?"

Startled and a bit disappointed, she realized that Blake was not going to show, and she knew that she could look forward to Leonard taking her someplace to relax in some beautiful atmosphere with interesting conversation. "I'd like that, Leonard." She was putting the last dish of food in the refrigerator, when Leonard rang the doorbell. She opened the door ready to leave. Leonard held his breath as he gazed at her. "I like your taste in clothing, Madam."

"You had better. It's a Velasco original."

Herman drove then to the Mitsukoshi Japanese Restaurant, and after being seated, Leonard ordered sushi. "The food here is delicious. You'll enjoy every morsel."

"If you like it, I'm sure that I will."

He beamed, and tried not to blush, but did, a little. He was enjoying himself and so was she, but she couldn't help thinking of Blake and wondering what had happened to him.

He glanced at her while sipping his champagne. "What's wrong, sweet?"

Somehow she wasn't surprised that he had noticed. Leonard never missed anything. She smiled and shrugged her shoulders. Never let a man know that you are thinking of another, especially while you are out with him." "I was thinking about the D. C. shop."

"God, you are so dedicated. What did I do to deserve you?" He took her hand and brought it to his lips. "Let's forget about the stores for tonight."

"Whatever you say, boss." She smiled into his eyes.

He pulled her closer and put this arm around her, and they sat like that for the rest of the evening, talking, laughing, and enjoying the food.

They finished dinner, and talked for a while over coffee, before he took her home. When Herman stopped in front of her home, Leonard turned her to him. "Thanks for tonight." He pressed a quick kiss on her lips.

When she entered her house the phone was ringing. She answered and heard an annoying voice. "Hi, babe."

A cold knot formed in her stomach. "What do you want, Sonny?"

"I want my family back."

He's suffering. Good, she thought. Nevertheless, she had to give it to him straight. "We're not the same people we were years ago. This is another day and time."

"Love never dies," he whispered in the phone.

"It does if one or the other kills it, and you killed it, Sonny."

"That was in the past."

"Ok. The mistake was made, it's over, and we go on with our lives, but separately."

"You love me. Admit it. Let's rekindle the flame that once burned within you," he said. "Look deep, remember, and stop fighting it."

"I knew you were immoral, but I never suspected, till now, that you are insane."

"Ok, I see, you want me to win you back."

"It won't do you any good," she replied sharply.

"No, babe, we belong together. You're not getting rid of me that easily. We'll be together again."

"You vain, conceited impossible jerk!" She hung up on him. She went to bed thinking of what Sonny had said. In love with him? He's nuts.

The next morning, Dolores felt mentally and physically drained after tossing and turning half the night, and she could barely get ready for work. When she did get to work, Sonny was standing in her office. A swift shadow of anger swept across her face. "What's wrong with you? Coming here like this, and in my office?" She pushed past him.

"I have something to ask you." His voice was quiet and a glazed look of despair began to spread over his face.

"I have tons of work," she said angrily, and sat at her desk. "I can't talk to you now."

He started pleading, "I have to talk with you, please."

She slapped some sketches down on her desk and leaned back in her chair. "You have ten minutes."

"Let me come over and see my kids tonight."

"What makes you think they want to see you?" She rolled her eyes at him.

He sat in the chair by her desk, buried his head in his hands and wept, tears and snot running down his face.

"Oh for goodness sake." She handed him a tissue. Seeing him cry softened her feelings a little, and she put her hand to his shoulder. "Ok."

"Think they will ever forgive me?"

"Sure. They're wonderful kids. Come to dinner tonight." Then her thoughts shifted to Leonard. It would be awkward if he came to her office while Sonny was there blubbering all over her desk. She got up and pushed him toward the door. "See you tonight."

That evening after Dolores got home, Michelle had started dinner. "Prepare enough for five. Your daddy is eating with us and he eats a lot."

"Aw, Mom, I was going to the movies with my friends." There was a pensive shimmer in the shadow of her eyes. "Why tonight?"

"He said that he wanted to see you and James."

Sonny came at 6 o'clock. They sat down to eat with Sonny sitting next to Dolores and his children sitting across from them. James blessed the food and Sonny started eating.

"Delicious!" he said. "You're still a good cook."

"Michelle cooked most of it," James said, studying him with curious intensity.

Sonny smiled at Michelle and stated, "Just like your mama."

Michelle sneered at him, her face ringed with bitter resentment. "I had sixteen years of practice, starting at age ten."

Sonny fell silent, and his smile faded until James spoke.

"We've a large back yard with a pool. You should come for a barbecue sometime."

"I could come one__."

Dolores interrupted, "I'm sure your daddy will be too busy to bother with us, besides you kids are never home."

Sonny glanced sadly at Dolores and continued to eat.

After dinner, Sonny and Dolores went to the living room and the children followed, but sat on the opposite end of the room. Michelle wasn't moved by her daddy's confession of sorrow, but James felt compassion for him. "Did you have to be nasty to Daddy at dinner," he whispered to Michelle.

"I was letting him know that we don't have room in our lives at this late date."

"He made a mistake. We should give him a chance."

"Butt out!" She yelled. "You don't understand any of it."

"Do so!" He yelled back. "He's trying to give us what we missed."

"Oh, yeah! That's all you care about," she said and bumped his knee with hers. "You want to wear fine clothes."

"Leave me alone," James said, his face turning red.

"I'll say it again," she declared. "I don't need him and neither do you."

"Are you kids getting bored?" Dolores asked.

Michelle arose. "We would like to be excused."

Ok," she said, grateful to Michelle for saying that."

They said goodbye to Sonny and went upstairs leaving her and Sonny alone. Sonny gazed at Dolores, sitting alone on the sofa, aloof, cold and stern. "I wish that I could hold you in my arms like before on those wonderful nights we spent together."

"Those days are gone forever."

"If I could have a second chance, everything would be different."

"Sometimes there are no second chances in life."

"Can't we try?"

"It's no use in rehashing old dreams." Dolores glanced at the clock on the wall.

"It's late," he said. "I'd better get back to the hotel." He left and twenty minutes later, while opening the door to his hotel room, his phone rang."

"Daddy? James here. Come for breakfast tomorrow."

"Will it be ok with your mother and Michelle?"

"Mom says it's okay. Don't mind Michelle. She'll come around. Come before 10 o'clock."

Sonny placed the phone on the nightstand next to his bed. "There is hope for us," he murmured. "Things are looking up."

The next morning, Sonny was knocking on Dolores' door at 9:45. Dolores opened the door and let him enter. "You're just in time. We're ready to eat." They went to the dining room and Dolores motioned for Sonny to sit at the head of the table. He smiled and tears glistened in his eyes. While eating, they talked of what they were going to do in the summer.

Sonny joined in the conversation. "I want to start a car dealership in another state. New York, maybe."

Michelle and James stared at each other. Then James asked, "Would you move to New York?"

"I'd like to be near my family," he answered and his eyes shifted from one to the other, trying to read the expression on their face.

"You aught to give it a try," James said.

"You're a glutton for punishment," Michelle whispered in his ear. "You want your way no matter whom it affects."

"Mom seems pleased," James noted, watching Dolores' expression. "They did love each other once."

"No longer," Michelle snapped. "She despises him and so do I."

"We will see. Maybe having him back might not be so bad."

"Never!" she said and excused herself from the table.

Dolores, Michelle and James saw Sonny everyday for two week until he returned to Berkeley.

Michelle and James couldn't wait to get back with their friends, and Dolores was home alone. She phoned Leonard. "What's happening?"

"I know that tone in your voice," he said. "Did something happen to upset you?"

Sonny was here for two weeks."

"Sonny?" He sounded like someone with a frog stuck in his throat. "Are you two getting back together? What about that Blake fellow? Is Sonny coming here to live?"

"He talked of opening a car dealership here. He's doing well."

"How would that set with you?" he asked, trying to get some perspective of her feelings.

"Wouldn't care one way or the other. It has nothing to do with me."

"I feel a little at ease, but I heard that Sonny could charm a Rattlesnake. You're not planning on leaving the stores are you?"

"Are you kidding? Never. I love my job."

"Ok. I believe and trust what you're telling me. Otherwise, my life and business would be ruined."

"You have nothing to worry about. I would never leave you for Sonny."

They talked for two hours, until she got sleepy.

"Get some rest, sweet. You're leaving for Washington tomorrow."

Dolores slept until noon and got up to add some last minute clothing to her suitcase. She was ready when Leonard came for her. "I have your tickets and reservations," he said. "Hattie will stay with the children and I will look in when she needs me."

"You're such a blessing." She kissed him and boarded the plane, and after arriving at Washington

Reagan Airport, She phoned Leonard. "What's my favorite guy doing?"

"Eating some of a spectacular beef roast," he answered.

"Oh, my salivary glands are secreting! She made a licking sound with her tongue.

"Order some dinner, have fun, don't work hard, Dolores."

"Can't without you," she said softly.

"Oh, Ms. Brown, I love how you talk."

They said goodbye and Dolores went to bed.

Early Friday morning, she went to the shop on F Street, North West. Mr. Paul Seitz, the manager let her enter. "It's early, Ms. Brown."

"That's the way to get ahead, Mr. Seitz."

He coughed, cleared his throat and said, "Uh__yeah, you got a point." He took the microphone off his desk and made an announcement on the intercom. "All employees to the conference room, STAT."

When everyone was seated, Mr. Seitz called attention. "This here's Ms. Dolores Brown. You know why she's here."

"Thanks, Mr. Seitz. Fellow employees, we are going to change this store's image." She brought the microphone closer. "The way we handle clientele, our line of fashion and selling techniques will all change."

Dolores was in Washington for three months before returning home. Leonard met her at the airport. "The transformation was a success. The customers went for our fashion ideas."

"You've done it again, sweet. I want you to go home and rest."

Chapter Six

Michelle was a senior in high school, and graduation was nearing. "Mom, the prom is two week away. Can we shop for my dress?"

"Let's do it Saturday. I'll have more time." Several buyers were due at Velasco's. Dolores was too busy to shop, and rest was what she wanted when she came home from work.

Michelle talked about her dress all week, and that Saturday, tired as Dolores had been, she drove Michelle to town. They walked for hours, browsing in and out of six different dress shops until they walked into Saks Fifth Avenue. "Mom? That dress! It's what I want."

"Thank God!" Dolores sank in a chair outside the dressing room. "My feet were doing some serious talking to me."

Michelle took the dress from the rack and held it in front of her. "It's perfect."

"Good. Try it on, get it wrapped and let's get out of here." Dolores stared at the dress and got an idea. "Velasco's should offer clothing for your age" She was still in thought when Michelle tried the dress and danced out of the fitting room.

"This color is just right for our prom theme." She popped her fingers and moved about.

"This isn't the dance floor," Dolores said. "Linen shoes can be dyed to match that dress."

"Smart idea, Mom."

"Ok. Give the dress to me and I'll pay for it while you get dressed."

That Monday, following the weekend of shopping with Michelle, Dolores was tired but she went to work. Leonard came into her office in a cheerful mood. "Have you listened to the birds singing outside your window and smelled the aroma of the fresh spring air?"

She laughed and said, "You're in a happy mood this morning."

"I have to shop for a few graduations." He whistled and threw his hands in air.

"Do you know anyone graduating this year?"

"Just Michelle. She will be devastated if you forget her."

Darn!" He slapped his cheek. I'll be devastated if I forget that one." He turned on his heels and strode to the door to catch the elevator down.

Leonard didn't return to the office, and when the workday ended, Dolores went home.

Dolores was about to take a bath and to get comfortable when the phone rang. Leonard was on the line apologizing. "Sorry about staying away all day. I had a lot of shopping to do."

"Leonard, don't tell me you bought the store," she said, teasing.

"I've got to make my ladies happy. I'll be there to take a picture of Michelle in her prom dress."

"Your approval means a lot to her."

Dolores spent all day getting Michelle ready for the prom. Come Friday, she was rushing around, seeing to all of the particular last minute details before Michelle got dressed. 7 o'clock had rolled around and Michelle was still in the mirror applying her makeup. Dolores entered her bedroom "Bill is downstairs. He's getting jittery. Better hurry."

Leonard had also arrived and was waiting to see Michelle in her dress. Dolores took Michelle's hand and ushered her to the stairs. Michelle floated and bounced down one step at a time. Her ash brown hair clustered in long curls bounced around her face. She had used coloring just for the prom. Her beauty was exquisite, fragile and overwhelming.

Bill met her half way and escorted her down, grinning, not taking his eyes off of her. "You look beautiful."

"Thanks, Bill, and you're bumping in your tux." She smiled; aware of the captivating effect she'd made descending the stairs.

Bill straightened his bow tie and his grin widened, showing all of his front teeth and gums.

Before letting them leave, Leonard gave a little speech and advice. "Don't rush, obey the speed limit, watch out for the other guy, and no speed racing."

Dolores touched his arm, "Leonard, they have to leave."

"Don't worry, Mr. Velasco, I'm a boss driver."

Yeah, Uncle Leonard, don't worry," she said, took Bill's arm and hurried out to his car.

Leonard and Dolores watched them drive away.

Several hours had passed since Michelle and Bill had left. It was past midnight. Dolores and Leonard sat in the kitchen drinking coffee. They were on their fifth cup when a car drove into the driveway.

Michelle ran into the kitchen. "Bill and I had it all. A boss dinner, champagne__."

"Whoa, young lady! Champagne?" Leonard threw his hands in air.

"Uncle Leonard, it was just a small glass." She described the size and measure of the glass with her thumb and first finger.

"There shouldn't be any drinking on prom night. Was this before or after dinner?"

"Dinner is always before the prom, Uncle. Didn't you do that in your day?"

"No," he answered, remembering his first prom. "We had chaperones."

She made a face and said, "That must've been ages ago."

Dolores put her hand over her mouth to prevent laughing.

Leonard said, "It wasn't that long ago."

"Uncle Leonard!" She exclaimed and went on to tell more of what had occurred at the prom.

"It's close to 3 o'clock," Dolores said. "Let's finish this conversation at breakfast."

I'm not eating breakfast," Michelle informed her, going up the stairs. "A girl has to watch her figure."

Leonard exchanged a smile with Delores and shook his head. "Were you ever that way?"

"Not me. I was the carefree type."

"I'm happy that she had a great time," Leonard said. "See you at the office."

Two weeks after graduation, Michelle wanted to go shopping again, this time for a college wardrobe. Dolores was getting ready for work when she entered her bedroom, sat beside her and put her arms around her shoulders. "Mom, I'm a young lady, and I appreciate the fact I'm able to attend college."

"What is it now?" she asked, irritably, trying to get ready for work.

"I need money for clothes," she answered, closing her eyes, waiting for Dolores' explosive answer.

Dolores stared at her for a long moment, and then said, "You can have the money tomorrow."

Michelle let out a yell, hugged Dolores and left the room.

Dolores got to work; Leonard was sitting behind her desk. He smiled widely, showing most of his ivory-capped teeth. "Take a business trip with me."

"Where?" she asked, tingling with anticipation.

"Hawaii," he answered, grinning mischievously.

You're full of surprises today. What's up?"

He shifted in the chair, leaned back with his long arms resting behind his neck. "There's a showing on fashions, fabrics and makeup, what's new in the market and __."

"I used to dream of going there. That would be a great vacation." She was all for going until she thought of Blake. "May I let you know later?"

"Sure," he answered, disappointed at her hesitation. "Think it over."

She had done a lot of thinking for the past few months, with no decision, particularly about Blake, and she thought she had better talk to him before leaving on any trips. The phone rang, as she was about to place a call.

"Sorry I missed out date," Blake said, his voice sounding shaky.

My best friend had an accident."

"That's alright. I understand."

"I should have called you but it just wasn't possible."

The sincerity of his apology assured her that he had not meant to treat her badly. "I'm not angry. I assumed that you were detained for some reason."

"What about next weekend?" he asked. "I miss your good cooking. "Would you happen to have saved any for me?"

"Sorry. All gone. I'm leaving for Hawaii," she said, deciding in that instance. Maybe the trip would help her to come to some decision about Blake, and maybe she had already decided, but needed to convince herself.

"We haven't made our plans," he said, his voice uncompromising, yet gentle.

"I'll be gone for two weeks. We have plenty of time."

He groaned softly, and then sounded desperate. "That's too long. Miss me a lot."

"Every moment," she said and sent him a kiss through the phone.

Dolores told Leonard at lunch that she was going to Hawaii.

He sprang to life. "It won't be all business. I promise." He went to his office whistling and singing. An hour later, he returned with plane tickets and put them in her hand. "Ready for fun in the sun?"

"You've got me hyped. I couldn't stay home now if you paid me."

"Take the rest of the day off. Go home and pack. I'll call you later."

Dolores left the office, but headed for the beauty salon, had her hair set, and then went shopping. Three hours later, she went home to pack, spend time with Michelle and James, and then got ready for bed.

7 o'clock, the next morning, the phone awakened her. "Leonard? Yeah? 9 o'clock? I'm ready." It was 8:30 when she got out of bed and hurried to dress. The flight was scheduled to leave at 11 o'clock and knowing Leonard's rule of being on time, always prevailed. She was pushing it.

Herman was outside her door at 9 o'clock. He put her bags in the car and got them to the airport at 10 o'clock. Leonard checked the bags and they still had time for anything else. "Let's have coffee till it's time to board," he suggested, taking her arm and heading for the eatery. They sat, drinking, not saying anything. Then he said, "The first time I met you and later, I've been wild about you." He held her hand. "Week after week, wanting you, twisted me into such a state that was tearing at my soul. I had to let you know how I've felt."

The call to board the plane came just as she opened her mouth to say something. They boarded the plane and were seated comfortably. Now, she had to think of what she was going to say to him, but he spoke first.

"I would like to have a partner for all of my stores."

"You're bringing others into the business?" she asked, beckoning the steward for a drink. Everything was happening so fast and she needed a drink to calm her nerves.

"One person," he answered. "If she is interested."

A female, she thought. How was this going to affect her position? She had better find out now. "When do you plan on asking her?"

"Like now," he answered. "Would you consider coming in with me?"

She swallowed hard, nearly choking on the ice in her mouth.

Leonard slapped her back until she had finished coughing. "I need someone who is trustworthy, and who better else than you."

Too many things were happening, and she let her suspicions be known. "Is this because of Sonny or Blake?"

He admitted his fears, "Sonny and Blake are fast talkers. I don't want to lose you."

"Sonny and I were married for five years. I loved him, but it's over."

"What about that Blake fellow?"

Bracing herself for his reaction, she answered, "He's given me an engagement ring."

His face appeared tense but he acted cautiously, hesitated for a moment, and then asked, "Do you know anything about this man? His life, culture, or principles? Where did he come from?"

"Don't look at me like that. I didn't say that I would marry him. We talked, but no plans have been made."

"I'm sorry if my blowing off steam upset you, but I love you, Dolores." He put his arm around her.

"Why didn't you tell me before? You could've made all of this easy."

I was afraid. I didn't think that you wanted me," he answered. "I am ten years older than you."

She touched his chin and shook it with her fingers. "Silly, I've always admired and respected you."

"But can you love me?"

Dolores blinked her eyes, then gazed at him for a few minutes. There was something about Leonard that was indescribable, and he did make her laugh. They had become close friends and he had taught her how to live. She found herself answering him earnestly, "I could love you absolutely and completely for the rest of my life."

He grinned and asked, "What are we going to do about it?"

"Let's be together forever."

"I figured that I had to take you away where no one could plead their case before I pled mine."

"You sly devil!" she said and hit him affectionately. "You planned this trip."

"Fasten your seatbelt, sweet, we're about to land," he said and laughed.

The plane landed in Hawaii at 3:00 a.m. Dolores and Leonard got two adjoining rooms in the Sheridan Waikiki Hotel. "I'm going to hit the sack," Dolores said and yawned, "Wake me later."

"Yes, sweet," Leonard said and kissed her.

It was noon when Leonard walked into Dolores' room. "Wake up my beauty. Let's have lunch." He leaned down and kissed her, and she parted her lips to accept his deepening kiss.

Desire flooded her loins and she thought she had better show some restraint and she pulled away. "I'll get dressed. Meet you downstairs?"

Leonard let out a wistful sigh, straightened up and left her room.

They had lunch in the hotel and drank a round of Mai Tais. Then, Leonard told her what he had planned. "We'll take a plane ride to Oahu. My friends have good things in store for us."

"This is exciting," she said and smiled.

"We'll shop for rings tomorrow. I have a friend who makes jewelry."

She laughed, softly, and laced her fingers with his. "What are we getting?"

"He's making special rings for us," he answered, grinning down at her, his eyes shining with love for her.

"Let's have an inscription," she suggested.

"He agreed, "What's the inscription?"

"Leonard and Dolores, in love forever." She slid her arms around his neck.

He wrapped his arms around her, drew her closer and guided her face up to his for a kiss. They walked arm and arm into the store and began to look at pictures of rings, and an hour later; they had chosen two diamond cut gold bands.

"Come back in three hours," said his friend, the jeweler.

They walked around Ala Moana Shopping Center until it was time to get the rings, and later, they went to get their blood tested.

"I must call Michelle and James," she said.

We can call them from Oahu," he said. They went back to the hotel, packed a few clothing and went to the airstrip. When they landed in Oahu, Leonard's friend, Howard, met them. They embraced and he introduced Dolores. Howard kissed her and she was impressed when he drove them to his home. "A house overlooking the beach. Incredible scenery."

"That is why I had to bring you," he said, looking out over the crystal blue Pacific waters.

Delores and Leonard walked inside the garden lined with wild tobacco, beautiful palm trees, emerald lantana shrubs and white orchids. Howard's wife greeted them and directed them to a seat on a mat on the grass. She waved her hand and the music started. Young, beautiful women ran in front of them and lay their Lau hala mats on the grass with lala' au dance sticks. They performed the hula and invited Dolores to participate, and she moved her hips and her hands to the music. "I'm getting the hang of it," she called to Leonard.

"Exotic!" he called back to her. Watching her move seem to intensify his wanting her. "I have to control my desires," he mumbled under his breath. "Waiting would be worth it."

Dolores laughed and continued to dance. When the music stopped, she landed beside Leonard. He handed a glass of champagne to her, drew her close and put his arm around her and tenderly kissed her lips. "We'll have a traditional Hawaiian ceremony."

"Wonderful," she whispered and pressed her lips to his.

It was 1 o'clock in the morning when they went to their rooms. Delores lay in bed thinking about her wedding and suddenly thought about Blake. There could be no marriage without talking to him. What if he's asleep? No matter. She had to call him. She stood awkwardly in the middle of the room with the phone in her hand. What was she going to say? She slowly dialed his number and waited for him to answer. The phone rang four times. "Pick up!" She murmured quietly. He answered on the sixth ring and she froze for a moment and then spoke, "Blake?"

"Hi, darling. I miss you."

"I've got something to tell you."

"Are you ready to become my wife?" He interrupted her, his voice hardy and he chuckled.

How was she going to tell him without hurting him? There was no way but to come right out with it. "I'm sorry, Blake. Leonard proposed and I accepted."

"Why him and not me, Dolores?"

"Leonard has been my soul mate through trying times. He loves me."

"I love you, too," He said in a grudging voice.

"I don't mean to hurt you, but I have loved him for years and I didn't realize it till now."

Blake spoke in a weak and tremulous whisper, "Be happy, Dolores. That's all I've ever wanted for you."

"Thanks, Blake." She put the phone on the table, breathed deeply and lay back in bed. Blake's pride had been hurt, but he was a survivor. He would move on, find someone else the way he found her. She wouldn't be surprised if he had someone in mind already.

The next morning, after eating breakfast, Dolores called Michelle and James. Michelle answered the phone, "Mom, how's it going?"

"Leonard has asked me to marry him."

"Mom, that's great. He's the best."

"You don't mind?"

"Heck no. I love Uncle Leonard."

"Thanks, sweetheart. Tell James the news, and I'll see you in two weeks." Two hours later, Dolores was getting ready for her wedding.

Howard's wife, Tralana, was hemming her white English lace wedding dress to fit Dolores, while their neighbors made a tiara of fresh pink carnations, jasmine, pink orchids, and white and yellow ginger for her head.

Howard fitted Leonard with his traditional suite that he wore when he married Tralana. It was 2 o'clock when Dolores marched through a row of silver sword that had hundreds of yellow and magenta-hued flowers, and dozens of beautiful white orchids with lavender tops. Leonard took his place beside her; they began their vows, and were pronounced man and wife by the priest of Kahulni. They signed their marriage license. "I've never been this happy," Leonard said, his luminous hazel brown eyes shining with love. They shared a kiss that left them both breathless and neither of them wanted it to end, but he let go of her and they walked briskly and happily down the path toward the beach where the celebration had been prepared for them. Dolores sniffed the air, "Hmm, what a delicious aroma."

They sat in wicker high back chairs that had been decorated with red hibiscus, plumeria and tuberoses. Huge firelights were staked in the sand, and along with a bright moon, that made a romantic setting.

Leonard uncorked the champagne, poured two glasses and handed one to Dolores. She sipped the Moet and Chandon and he drank his hurriedly. Then Howard led them to the food. There were sweet and sour chicken, whole fish with bean curd and vegetables, lobster Szechuan, poi, fresh fruit and macadamia nut cake. All of these delicacies might have been sand for all the attention Leonard gave to the food. His eyes were on Dolores, and he could hardly wait to take her in his arms to make love to her. "Let's eat and get out of here," he said kissing her neck.

"It's too early." We have to show our appreciation to Howard and Tralana, thirty minutes the most."

"Ok, but not a minute longer," he said and feathered kisses over her cheek.

The neighborhood band, that Howard had engaged, started playing and the men danced with Dolores while the women danced with Leonard. They danced, passing Dolores to the next man in line until she landed in Leonard's arms. She pressed closer to him and he groaned. "I'm dying," he said as their bodies swayed against each other. "I don't know how long I can sustain this torture. I need to make love to you."

Dolores slid her arms around is neck and pressed closer to him and their bodies moved as one, swaying in tune to the sensual rhythm. "Do you feel that?" She laughed and nibbled his ear.

A shutter ripped through him. His lust was mounting by the minute. "That does it," he said with a flushed and congested look on his face. "You're in trouble now."

A tremor passed through her and she whispered in his ear, "Take me to bed and make love to me now."

He picked up in his arms and took her to the room that had been prepared for them. She eased out of his arms, kicked her shoes off and untied the ribbons on her dress.

He unbuttoned his shirt, pulled it off his arms, and let it fall to the floor, his eyes never leaving her for an instant. He reached for her dress and lowered it slowly, gazing at her, taking in her long slim body, her curves, small flat stomach, tight breast and shapely nipples that stood outward. "You've got one hell of a body," he said picking her up and lowering her onto the bed. He came down on the bed, his body hard with desire, his hands stroking her tight round bottom until she was slick, hot and ready. Then he lifted her onto his body, spread her thighs with one of his own until her thick curly mound brushed the thickness of his loins. He entered her and began a slow steady movement.

Soon she matched her movements to his and she cried out as he plunged deeper when she arched her body closer to his. Her body began to convulse and he could feel the spasms tearing through her until he was rocked by the fiery sensation of his release.

He continued to hold her, stroking her most sensitive flesh and kissing her gently. "I've never known such ecstasy," she said, quivering with joy, opening her mouth and receiving his tongue and giving back her own.

He tore his lips from hers and gazed at her body and she felt like she was the most beautiful woman on earth.

"I want to remember this moment and how much I love you," he said. "You're like a flower unfolding for the first time."

The next morning, Leonard awakened Dolores with a kiss and breakfast in bed.

"You're going to spoil me," she said, rising to kiss him.

"Nothing is too good for my wife," he said receiving her kiss.

After breakfast, they got dressed, thanked Howard and Tralana, and flew back to the hotel.

Leonard had Dolores' clothing moved to his suite. The manager complimented them with lots of Mai Tais.

"A toast to my bride," Leonard said, holding the class in the air. "May we be forever in love as we are today."

"I'm never going to let you get away," she said, holding him tightly.

Leonard kept drinking and Dolores' head was spinning.

"No more," she said. "My glass looks like three. I'm seeing triple."

"Ok, my lovely. That's enough for tonight. Let's go to bed."

She smiled, wiggled her body and ran to the bed. He chased her, pulled her onto the bed beside him, and they made love until the early morning hours.

Later that day, Dolores and Leonard packed their bags and went to the Honolulu International Airport for the flight home. Before boarding, they phoned Michelle and James. "Mom, we're happy you called. Daddy is here with us."

"Yeah," James said, listening on the extension. "He's waiting for you to come home."

"We haven't told him that you're married," Michelle said. "It's going to be tough telling him."

"Hope he can handle it," James said. "All he talks about is getting you back."

"Sonny knows better. I'll see you tomorrow." What nerve Sonny has. He's going to be a member of this family his own way, she thought, going back to the waiting area.

"Everything all right, sweet?"

"No. Sonny is living at my house with the kids."

"Damn. I knew he was going to pull something." He angrily slammed the bags to the floor. "He's not giving up."

"Don't worry," she put her hands on his cheeks and kissed his lips. "We're married. What can he do?"

Chapter Seven

Herman met Dolores and Leonard at the airport and took them to Leonard's house. Dolores started unpacking and clearing a space in his closet for her clothes and thought of Sonny. "I've got to face the problem at home," she murmured aloud, resenting his intrusion into her life.

The next day, she and Leonard went to her house. She dreaded the confrontation that was soon to happen between Sonny and Leonard. When Herman drove into her driveway, they got out and stood before the front door. She slowly opened the door and stepped into the hall.

Sonny was standing in the living room. He stared at her then at Leonard. "What's happening, babe?"

"Leonard and I were married two weeks ago," she said, fixing her eyes on Sonny's face and bracing herself for his reaction.

Sonny's face darkened considerably. His jaw dropped then snapped shut in a tightening position. He gritted his teeth, his eyes blazed and he lashed out at Leonard. "Dirty bastard. You stole my wife when my back was turned."

Leonard folded his arms across his chest. There was no doubt he was equally as angry, and he yelled, "Deserter. You abandoned her."

Sonny drew a fist, and she stepped in between them. "I can't believe this. We've been divorced for eight years." She swung her fist in the air. "Oh, if I wasn't a lady I'd kick your ass."

Sonny calmed down and apologized, "God, I'm sorry. You didn't deserve that." He turned to Leonard. "Thanks for taking care my family." He held out his hand to Leonard, and Leonard shook his hand reluctantly. "I love you, Dolores, and I want you to be happy."

"I'm happy," she said putting her arms around Leonard.

Sonny's dreams of getting her back was shattered, his hopes flattened and his sense of loss overwhelmed him. He had lost her again and he said angrily, "Ok, if he's whom you want, fine!" He went toward the door then came back. "I would like to see my children often."

Dolores was furious and she started to argue but changed her mind. Something inside of her said no, think of Michelle and James. He was their father, and so she said, "You're welcome here because of our kids."

Sonny suddenly seemed ashamed of the way he had spoken and he said, "Thanks, babe, I won't take anymore of your time." He left, but not before glancing back at Leonard with a devious smile on his face.

Leonard was aghast. "Did you see that look on his face?" he asked. "He's up to something."

"What look," she asked, her brows lifting, looking puzzled.

"I'm telling you, he's planning something."

Forget him, honey," she said and called Michelle and James, who must have heard the argument but didn't enter the room.

James came through the living room door and threw his arms around Dolores "Mom, I'm so glad you're home."

"Good to have you home, Mom," Michelle said. "Hi, Uncle Leonard."

"You can delete the uncle bit. Your mother and I are married now."

"Oops! Forgot. You're our Dad now."

"Just make it Leonard for now. You can call me dad when you feel the need."

"Are you guys living here?" Michelle asked and introduced an important point they had yet to discuss.

She stared at Dolores and there was a moment of silence.

Then Dolores spoke, "There's room for all of us in our new home."

"I'll have Herman bring all of your clothing to the house tomorrow," Leonard said.

"We want to stay here," James said, stiffening, watching his mother's face.

"Absolutely not," Dolores said. "We're going to live together as a family."

Michelle tried to explain, "I'm a college student, and James is a high school senior. We want to be on our own."

"Nonsense." Dolores said, resenting the idea. "Alone in this house? I don't think so."

"You're upset," James said calmly.

"Upset?" She yelled at him, appalled that she was yelling. She had never raised her voice to her children in their life.

Michelle tried to appeal to Leonard, "Can you get Mom to see that we need privacy?"

Leonard glanced at Dolores standing with her arms folded and patting her foot. He wasn't about to say anything that would get her upset with him. "You can get all of the privacy you'll need at our house. I'll see to it."

"I thought you'd understand," Michelle cried. "We want our own home."

"Our home is your home," Leonard said. "We're a family now,"

"I won't stand for this attitude you're giving me." She rocked back and forth on her heels, and walked back and forth from Michelle to James.

"Let's discuss this tomorrow," Leonard said. "Sleep on it."

It was 7 o'clock the next morning. Dolores was getting ready for work when the phone rang. "An accident? Yes. I know Sonny Brown." She sat on the bed for a minute, and then frantically called Leonard. He ran to her looking around the room.

"What's wrong, sweet?"

"Sonny has been hurt. He's in New York Memorial Hospital."

"Wake the children. I'll call Herman."

They got in the car and when Herman pulled up in front of the hospital, they got out and ran inside. Sonny's doctor was attending to him.

"Are you Dr. Nichols," Dolores asked, acting as if she would pass out from shock.

"Yes. Your husband's back was injured close to his spine."

"Will he walk again?" she asked, not correcting him when he referred to her as his wife.

"It'll be a while. I had to operate to straighten two dislocated disks. He's unconscious."

Tears flooded Michelle's face and James held onto her, struggling to hold back tears. He had always tried to be the man of the family.

Michelle looked down at her father. "Wish I hadn't been mean to him."

Leonard put his hand on her shoulder. "Your daddy will pull through."

She turned and held onto Leonard. "I can't leave him here."

"Don't worry. We'll get a room and stay the night."

They were allowed to spend the night, and early the next morning, Dr. Nichols came and talked to them. "Mr. Brown has regained consciousness. He's in traction. I'm recommending therapy later."

They hurried to Sonny's room. Michelle whispered in his ear, "Daddy, can you hear me?"

Sonny groaned and opened his eyes slowly and James bent over him. "What happened, Daddy?"

Sonny appeared dazed, and didn't answer.

"Do you know what happened," Dolores asked.

"No," he answered feverishly. "I was driving and I woke up here."

Dolores left the room to talk with Dr. Nichols. "Will Sonny be all right?"

"Mr. Brown will be here for two week, after that, he will need rest and therapy."

Dolores returned to Sonny's room. "When your father is released, he will need care."

"I'll care for Daddy till it's time to go back to school," Michelle said. "He'll stay in the house with James and me."

Dolores couldn't say no, but she wondered, was Michelle serious about caring for Sonny, or was this her chance to get her own way to stay in the house? "It's going to take a lot of work. Are you sure you can take care of him."

"I can do it, Mom."

"I'll help," James said, holding Sonny's hand, starring down at him and then at Dolores. "We can do it."

Two weeks later, Sonny left the hospital and was taken by ambulance to the house. A physical therapist visited once a week, but Michelle and James were doing most of the care. Sonny wouldn't do anything to help himself, and soon, Michelle and James became a nervous wreck. Dolores was concerned.

"Sonny has given up completely, and he is taking it out on our kids."

"It will all be over soon," Leonard said, hopefully. "He should be out of bed any day now."

A month had passed and Sonny had rented a wheelchair, still insisting that he couldn't walk.

Michelle had a date that evening, and was hoping for a break. Dolores was helping her to get ready. Sonny wheeled himself into her room. "Where're you going?"

"My boyfriend wants to see a movie and to have dinner later."

"That's it, get rid of me," he complained. "James went out. Now you're leaving?"

Dolores confronted him, angrily, "Don't you start that mess. You're not being fair to her and James. They've been with you since you left that hospital."

"You're right," he said, feigning pain. "Have a good time. I'm letting my condition get me down."

Michelle's face displayed a look of guilt that seemed to have made her feel uneasy and she relented. "I'll call Chuck and cancel the date."

"You'll do no such thing," Dolores said, and gave Sonny a hard cold stare. "I'll stay with him."

After that night, Dolores was caring for Sonny on weekends and sometimes during work hours. He looked forward to her coming and eating with him. "Feels like old times having you next to me."

"Don't get too comfortable," she warned. "This arrangement is over once you get out of that wheelchair."

"May not be for a while," he said. "I'm feeling weaker."

Another week had past, and Dolores' work at the store was piling up on her desk. Leonard became concerned. "You're not getting enough rest. You're tired most of the time. I don't like what's happening."

"I'm going to hire a nurse for Sonny," she said. "Everyone will be able to rest."

Leonard passed the phone book to her. "Do it now."

The nurse wasn't with Sonny for two weeks before he found fault with her. "She's not doing her job. Where is she when I need her?" He succeeded in getting rid of the nurse, and when Michelle started classes at New York University, Sonny constantly called James.

Leonard became suspicious. "Sonny has been in bed for two months. He's playing you, trying to get back into your life."

She agreed, "You're right. I'm going to give him enough time to play this episode out."

"You mean give the children time to see what's happening?"

"Yes. He even has them thinking twice."

"What are you going to do?" he asked.

"I'm going to straighten him out once and for all." She rang for Herman.

Herman drove Dolores to her house. She got out, unlocked the door and entered Sonny's room. He was watching television in bed. When he saw her, a smile creased his lips. "I knew you'd come today. My mind told me you'd come today. Happy you're here, babe."

Dolores' throat tightened and she paused, got a grip on herself, and then stated, "You won't be after you hear what I'm about to tell you."

"What's wrong, babe?" He raised himself up in bed.

"I want you out of this bed," she said pointing her finger at him. "Get yourself together, live your life and let our kids live theirs."

"That's easy for you to say. You got Leonard. Who've I got?"

"If you stop feeling sorry for yourself, you could find something and someone for you."

"Oh, sure. I'm supposed to forget our love and replace it with another?" he asked, raising his voice. "Maybe that was easy for you, but not for me."

"Don't lay that on me. You did it with drugs," she reminded him. "Do it again with something else."

"You're never going to let me live that down are you?"

"Find whatever it is you need," she said, ignoring his question. "If not, I'll have no choice but to place you in a nursing home."

He sprang forward, almost coming out of bed, staring at her, his eyes darting nervously back and forth. Waves of mounting fear seem to rush over him. He yelled, "No. You couldn't. What kind of life would I have without you? Tell me it's not too late to get you back?"

She felt weak in the knees and she sat heavily in the chair by his bed, but held firmly, starring him sternly in the eye and stating, "We are over. There are no more us." She clasped her hands in front of her and continued, "This is the first of May. You've got three weeks. Then I'm calling a nursing home to have them pick you up." She turned and walked out of the room, and when she got to the car, she was shaking, and she took a moment to compose herself.

"You ok, Mrs. Velasco?" Herman asked, gazing at her through the rearview mirror.

"Yes, Herman, let's get the hell away from here." She hoped that she had gotten through to Sunny. Never could she go through this a second time.

Dolores never went back to her first house again, and a week didn't pass without her checking on Sonny's progress. James and Michelle were happy to keep her informed, and Michelle asked, "Mom, what did you tell Daddy? He said that he never knew that you could be so tough."

"Tough?" Dolores asked and blew hard. "I learned, after living with him and his aunt Virginia."

It was the last of May. Sonny had moved out of Dolores' house, but he didn't go far.

One morning, a week later, Michelle phoned Dolores, "Mom? Daddy has bought the house across the street. He said that he wants to be near us."

"Which house across the street?"

"The one across from you and Leonard."

Dolores almost fell out of her chair.

This further inflamed Leonard. "That son of a bitch. I knew he's never going to give up on you."

Despite Sonny being across the street, they never came in contact until six months later. James was graduating from high school, and Sonny had asked to be seated with the family in the same row during the graduating exercises.

Dolores relented. "I've decided to be civil and polite to Sonny for our kids' sake." Once more they would have to see each other. 4:30 that evening, Leonard, Dolores and James were entering the school's auditorium when they saw Sonny drive up and park his Lincoln Town car. He came behind them, barreling through the door, looking anxious and sat next to Leonard. "Hi, Leonard___Dolores," he said, out of breath. "I thought I was late."

Leonard and Dolores nodded their head.

"Daddy?" James called and ran toward him. "I hoped you would be here."

"I wouldn't miss my son's graduation." He gave him a quick peck on the cheek. "You're almost as tall as me. Let me feel those muscles."

"Aw. Daddy. Quit your kidding," he said, laughing and tussling with Sonny.

Sonny smiled, his eyes filled with laughter and gazed at Dolores. "How've you been, babe?"

"Dolores frowned and said irritably, "Fine."

He waved his hand in the air. "I can't complain either. Everything is great."

"Seems as though he's gotten himself together," Leonard whispered in Dolores' ear.

Dolores glanced at Sonny. He was fashionably dressed in a beautifully cut navy silk suit, light-blue shirt and burgundy stripped tie with matching handkerchief in his lapel's pocket.

When Michelle entered and took a seat, Sonny got up and sat beside her. Dolores and Leonard sat on her right. When the graduation ceremonies started, Sonny sat there smiling and commented to Michelle, "James looks handsome in his cap and gown."

When the principal called James Brown, Sonny stood up and clapped. James went on stage to receive his diploma, and Sonny had tears in his eyes. He clapped and continued to do so until the next student's name was called. After the ceremonies, they went to dinner.

"I'm treating everyone to dinner if it's all right with you and Dolores," Sonny said.

"I don't mind," Dolores said.

James stared at Leonard, hoping he would agree.

"All right by me," Leonard said, not wanting to spoil it for James.

Sonny chose Jezebel's Restaurant on Ninth Avenue and Forty-fifth Street. "Ready for some southern soul food?" he asked, waiting to be seated. "Spareribs, fried chicken and garlic shrimp."

They all agreed, and were seated at a table for five. While they waited for their orders, Sonny talked about his business. "My business is booming. I'm adding BMW's to the lot." He smiled and glanced at Dolores. "That should bring a few thousand." He went on about how much money he was making and Dolores tried to contain herself. When they were served their food, She was hoping Leonard would finish eating as she was hurriedly eating hers. "I've got to get out of this restaurant," she whispered to Leonard. "He's making me sick."

"Who's up for dessert?" Sonny asked, viewing the menu.

Dolores quickly nodded, "No thanks. I'm stuffed."

The others followed Dolores and refused.

Well, I don't want to be the only one." He called for the check.

Dolores whispered to Leonard, "Glad he did that. "Let's go everybody. Thanks for dinner, Sonny."

James and Michelle waited until Sonny paid the check and walked out of the restaurant with him. "Want to hang out?" Sonny asked. "The night is still young."

"I promised to shoot pool with Julio," James said.

"I've got a date," Michelle said.

"Leonard and I have to get ready for work tomorrow."

"Goodbye, Daddy," James said.

When Dolores and Leonard got home, they were about to go to bed when the phone rang. Dolores kicked her shoes off, sat on the bed and answered. "Dr. Jones, here. Your mother had a stroke. She is unconscious. Get here as soon as you can." Dolores dropped the phone, and for a moment, she was shocked, and then she let out a shrill scream.

Leonard hurried from the bathroom and held her, trying to understand what she was saying.

"Mama Kate had a stroke," she said, choking back tears.

"I'll make reservations for four on the next available flight," he said. "It's times like this that I wish I had a private jet."

Six-thirty, that morning, they arrived in Berkeley. It was hot, a sweltering eighty degrees, but a gorgeous day, full of sunshine with a startling brilliance. Dolores shielded her puffy red eyes and got in the car that Leonard had leased.

When they arrived at Berkeley Hospital, Dolores went to Mama Kate's room and stood by her side. "I'm here, Mama." She held her hand in hers. "She looks pale and drawn."

Mama Kate's hair was silvery gray. She was now eighty years old. Her large frame appeared smaller and her mouth was twisted to the left side of her face. Dolores bent down and kissed her cheek. James and Michele did the same.

Mama Kate suddenly clutched Dolores' hand.

"She knows I'm here," she said and called her, "Mama?"

"Sometimes they can hear," Dr. Jones said. "In this case, it's just a reflex."

She shook her head, ignoring what Dr. Jones had said. "No. I believe my Mama knows I'm here. Mama, you know I'm here with you, don't you?"

Dolores stayed all night with Mama Kate, while Leonard, James and Michelle got a suite at the Sheraton Hotel. The next morning, when the nurse came to take Mama Kate's vital signs, she rushed out to call Dr. Jones. Dolores was asleep in the chair next to Mama Kate's bed when the doctor rushed into her room. "She's gone," he said listening to her heart with his stethoscope. "Must have passed during the night."

Dolores threw herself on Mama Kate's breast and cried, "I love you, Mama." When she was able to calm herself, she phoned Leonard, "Mama is dead."

"We're coming, sweet."

After the funeral, they stayed in Mama Kate's house, long enough to settle her financial affairs, and then flew back to New York.

Several weeks had passed since Mama Kate's death. It was now June the twelfth. "Tomorrow would have been Mama Kate's birthday," Dolores said, her voice shaking.

"I'm going to Paris to check on the models," Leonard said. "Hurley had a heart attack. Come with me."

"I'm not in the mood for Paris," she said somberly.

He took her in his arms and held her close. "Ok, sweet. You stay here and relax. I don't hope to be away no more than a week."

After Leonard had left, Dolores sat in the family room remembering the days gone by and drinking wine. It was 9 o'clock that night and she was still sitting and drinking wine, when she heard the front doorbell. "Jenny, get the door."

Jenny answered the door and let Sonny inside. "I've got to see Mrs. Velasco," he said.

Jenny showed him to the family room and left.

"Dolores arose from the sofa when she saw him. "Sit here." She handed him a glass of wine.

He sat down and took the wine. "Sorry about Mama Kate. You've had enough to deal with so I didn't tell you that I lost Aunt Virginia, last week."

"Virginia and I never had any love for one another, but I'm sorry she's gone." Her voice sounded thick with emotion and sorrow.

"She didn't hate you," he declared. "It was the Heroin talking most of the time."

Dolores heaved a wistful sigh. "We did have some damn awful fights." Then her eyes gleamed in warm remembrance as she confided, "But it wasn't all bad. We had happy moments."

"You were the bright spot in my life, Dolores. Before you, a family meant nothing to me," he held his head down. "I despised my Mother. She left me with Aunt Virginia. My Father? Well, he left when I was born."

A long, weary sigh slipped from Dolores, and she said, "It must have been hard for you growing up."

"Aunt Virginia helped some, but I was left to fend for myself."

She was tempted to touch him or comfort him in some way, but resisted the urge and glanced away as she sought to gain control of her emotions. "At least, you're happy now."

"Happy?" he gasped, his sad eyes roving over her lustfully. "Like hell I am."

"How can you not be? You're now a wealthy man."

He took her hand in his and stated, "A man can acquire all the riches he wants and still be miserable. Money can't take the place of love and family."

"Get some companionship. Even if you don't get married."

He gazed at her and declared, "The first time I met you, I fell in love." He kissed her hand. "Never had I experienced anything more wonderful or fulfilling than making love to you for the first time." He brought her hand to his cheek. "I can't think of any woman other than you."

She became distrustful, let go of his hand and stood. "Enough said about the past."

He didn't want to let go of her hand. He stood and continued, "You're so beautiful, babe. A woman like you comes along once in a lifetime." He quickly took hold of her.

She didn't sense him, didn't know that he was going to kiss her until she felt his strong arms around her and the warmth of his kiss on her lips. She trembled at the sensations he aroused, feelings that she once longed for. "Let go of me," she demanded, trying to turn, to yank free. "I knew I shouldn't have trusted you."

He held her arms clamped to her sides, but she was able to move away, yet the impression remained and blended with the memories of what they once shared together. She slowly inhaled a deep breath and exhaled, seizing her composure with all of her strength and intentions of setting him back on his heels.

With gentle care, he loosened his hold. "It's hard to control myself when I'm near you." He hurried toward the front door.

"Don't give me that. You knew what you were doing," she yelled. "I let you in, thinking we could have a decent conversation, and what did you do?"

"Remembering the past got to me, and I can't say it won't happen again. Make no mistake, babe, I want you back, and I'm not giving up."

"It's never going to happen." She grabbed his arm roughly, pushing him out of the door and clicking the latch.

Jenny stood behind her with the phone. "Mr. Velasco is calling."

Dolores stood still for a moment, thinking, then she took the phone and swore Jenny to secrecy, "Don't ever mention that Mr. Brown was here tonight. I couldn't bare Mr. Velasco knowing how foolish I was tonight."

"Yes, Ma'am," Jenny said and left the room quietly.

Dolores took a moment to compose herself, then slowly brought the phone to her ear and spoke cheerfully, "Hello, honey."

"Hi, sweet. Everything ok?"

"It is now. I miss you, darling."

"Me too," he said. "Worse yet, I'll be here another week. Hurley's gotten worse."

"Think you'll make it for James' College graduation?"

"I promise," he said.

James was graduating from Yale University Law School, and they had planned to go to Connecticut.

Leonard returned home before the week had ended, so that he could attend the graduation, but he was worried about the Paris shop. "Hurley can't manage the shop. His doctor's orders."

"Don't worry. We'll find someone. Let's get ready for the graduation.
"Is Michelle coming?"

"That tyrant of a boss wouldn't let her off for her brother's graduation."

"Ass -hole," he said. "I ought to call him and tell him so."

"Forget it, honey. She just got the job."

"Even so, he needs me to deal with him."

Leonard and Dolores flew to New Haven, Connecticut. When they arrived on campus, rooms had been set up for the parents, and early the next morning, the day of graduation, they had breakfast with James in the school's cafeteria. Later, James took them to Harkness Tower to look down on the campus.

"This beauty reminds me of home," Dolores said. "Too bad Michelle couldn't be here to see this."

"Yes, great scenery," Leonard said, looking down with his arms around her and James. "Exciting having a son receiving a law degree here, huh?"

James beamed at the thought of them being so proud of him. "Want to see the campus museum?" He led them out of the tower. "The Art Gallery is the oldest in the U.S."

After touring the museum, they went to the graduation ceremonies. Sonny was seated one row in front. He glanced back and nodded his head, and Dolores pretended not to notice him.

After graduation, James announced his intentions, "I want to practice law in Hartford, Connecticut."

"Why not New York?" Dolores asked, trying to understand his reasoning.

"Too many corporate lawyers," he answered, hoping she wasn't going to try and persuade him to return home. "I can do better in Hartford."

"Have you really looked into this, James?" She asked. "This doesn't seem to be a good plan."

"Yes," he answered, laconically.

"Ok, find a good location," Leonard said. "I'll buy an office for you. Consider this your graduation gift."

James flashed a huge smile and threw his arm around Leonard's shoulder. "This could be my chance to make it big."

Sonny stood silent during the conversation, but he wasn't going to let Leonard outdo him and he stated, "I'll throw in the furniture."

"Thanks, Daddy."

Later that day, Leonard and Dolores flew back to New York. Michelle met them at the Kennedy Airport. While driving home, Leonard voiced his concerns about the Paris shop. "I've got to find someone to take Hurley's place."

"Let me," Michelle said. "I made all A's in business."

Leonard thought for a moment then said, "I can get someone to train you."

She became excited. Her hands were flailing the air, and she said, "You don't know what this means to me."

"You would have to live in Paris," Dolores said. "Do you think you could do that?"

"What could be better? Magnificent night life, best food in the world, not to mention the greatest fashions."

"It's more than that," Dolores cautioned her. "You would have to keep the models in line, do volume sales, keep up with marketing trends and make sure we remain in the black."

"Is that something you can handle?" Leonard asked.

"That would be clock work for me," she replied, sounding sure of herself.

"Then it's settled. Take as much time as you'd like to prepare for the trip."

"No. I want to leave right away." The next few days were busy for Michelle. She and Dolores spent three days shopping at Velasco's. Michelle had chosen several silk suits of tailored simplicity in various colors of green, pink, muted beige, brown and pale blue. "What do you think?" She asked Dolores, posing in front of the mirror in the pale blue outfit.

"You're going to look like a woman in charge," Dolores answered, laughing gaily. "This suit was made for you and the color is flattering."

Dolores put her arms around her, kissed her cheek, then drew back and stared at her. She couldn't help noticing how she had grown into such a beautiful young woman, much like her. Her figure was shaped like an hourglass and her legs were slender and shapely.

Michelle looked pleased and returned her mother's kiss. "Thanks, Mom.

Chapter Eight

Michelle left New York, bound for Paris. Dolores was feeling lonely with all of her children gone. She had thrived on their well—being and they did need her constant supervision, though they were good kids. With all of this she used to think that she had more than enough to keep her fully occupied with her running the business and keeping the models in line. Lord knows Julienne was more than enough to keep her adrenaline pumping; but now, even the shop was no longer challenging. Everyday, she strode into the office with less pep in her step and acted as if the place had become secondary to everything else in her life.

Leonard thought he had better do something to cheer her. "Let's take a vacation. Tahiti sounds great for this time of year."

Dolores perked right up. "We can see Bora Bora, Bali hai, Moorea, Raiatea," she went on. "That would be fun."

"Book us on the Majestic Explorer Cruise Line," he said, pleased that she wanted to go.

The morning of the cruise was radiant with spring sunshine and a blue sky that was without a single cloud. Dolores took a deep breath and peered out of her bedroom window. New buds were beginning to sprout on her pink rosebushes, the weeping willow tree swayed under the cool fluttering breeze bringing the sweet scent of Jasmine planted at the edge of the lawn.

Leonard came behind her, held her for a moment and gave her a quick kiss on her neck. "Hurry and get dressed, sweet, we've a plane to catch to get to the ship."

"Yes, honey," she said and hurried to the shower.

When they had arrived in Tahiti, Leonard had planned a trip exploring the coral beaches, lush valleys and secluded villages. It was like a second honeymoon for them. Over the next few weeks, they had fun snorkeling and lying in the sun. Dolores walked along the beach, gazing out at the endless blue waters, while Leonard had fun on the golf course. They had spent three glorious weeks on the cruise. "Tomorrow is our last day here," Leonard said.

"I'd like to stay here forever," Dolores said.

"We do have a business to run," Leonard reminded her then kissed her.

"Yes," she said and sighed. "A business for which I am grateful to have."

When Dolores and Leonard arrived in New York, they left written instructions for Jenny not to disturb them, and they were late sleeping when Dolores was awakened by a thumping noise. She got out of bed to investigate, and after searching several rooms, came to the last one near hers. The door was ajar, a little, when she looked inside, hurried back to her room and flopped on her bed.

Leonard sat instantly up in bed. "What's wrong?" He rubbed his eyes and stared at her.

"James is in the next bedroom with some floozy," she answered, angrily. "She had her big legs wrapped around his body."

"Tell them that they have to sleep in separate rooms," Leonard said, with an irate look on his face. "We can't have them behaving like that in here."

"I should've told them that instead of coming back to bed." She got out of bed and hurried back to knock on their door.

"Yes," James called from his bedroom.

"Come out here," Dolores said, angrily.

James opened the door a crack and gazed into her angry eyes, and quickly announced, "I got married last night. You weren't here when we came home."

Her mouth flew open and she was unable to speak for a second. She felt guilty for misjudging them. He kept smiling, waiting for her to say something. Finally she said, in a mute voice, "Congratulations!"

Then in the next instance, Dolores exploded. "Why didn't you invite us to your wedding?"

He was unable to meet her gaze and stared at the floor. "I didn't want to see the hurt this may have caused you. We eloped." He continued to stare at the floor then called his wife, "Zola?"

She came to the door and embraced Dolores. "Nice to meet you, Mom."

Dolores felt quite affronted. She pulled away and called to Leonard, "Come and meet the newly weds."

Leonard wiped the sleep from his eyes and got his robe from the closet. "Did I hear correctly?" He stared at James and Zola.

"Aren't you going to say something?" James asked, smiling.

Leonard stuttered and quickly said, "the best to both of you."

Leonard and Dolores returned to their bedroom, still feeling shocked and uncertain as to what had just taken place. "He's got a lot of explaining to do," Dolores said, rattling the headboard on the bed. "How dare he get married without telling us first." She pounded her pillar and lay back. "We're still a family." She pulled the covers around her body in an angry gesture.

Everyone slept until noon. Around 1 o'clock, James and Zola joined them for lunch. James and Zola sat at the table with their arms around each other. Then James said, "Mom, Zola and I would like to live in the old house."

Dolores tried to control her anger, but James knew that her temper was raising the instant she spoke, "What happened, James, to your office, to your practice? What's this?"

He drew a quick breath, gazed sadly at her and at Leonard. "It didn't work out. I couldn't get my business going."

"You got married and you don't have a job?" Dolores asked. "You've got some nerve."

He could feel her angry stare, and he kept his eyes on Zola. "I can get one here." He kissed Zola and kept his eyes on her.

Zola laughed and returned his kiss.

Dolores ran her eyes over Zola's body, and she couldn't hold her tongue any longer. "What's the rush to get married? Are you pregnant?"

Zola held her mouth taught, jumped out of James' arms and stood wide legged. "Look at this body. Think I'd ruin this fine frame with a baby?"

Dolores stared at her deep brown hair that had the look of the best mink, long and silky, and thrust behind her ears, exposing large gold earrings. Her smoky brown eyes were like a cat's with a come hither look that spelled trouble. She was five feet ten inches tall without her shoes. A rose colored, full mouth sent one message, and her long slender body, clad in tight, silk pants, sent another. She emphasized her ass and then her tits with a sheer low cut blouse that mused Dolores.

When she walked, you could see every muscle and shape of her frame, and every time she moved, James' eyes followed her as though he was in a hypnotic trance.

A sexy, crafty slut, thought Dolores, and she was itching to tell her what she thought of her. "What motivated you?" She sounded scornful and suspicious.

Zola laughed hard, ran her fingers through James' hair and answered, "I want to be somebody, a model, rich and famous."

"I should spank you," James said, laughing. "Beautiful, young, sexy thing."

Leonard watched, not believing the way they were talking and acting. "Our shop models aren't rich or famous. We pay three thousand a month plus medical."

"That's a start," she said smugly. "That'll do for now."

"Yeah?" Dolores said sarcastically. "We will see."

James laughed, picked Zola up and carried her on his shoulder, spanking her lightly on her buttock as he climbed the stairs to return to their bedroom.

"She's a trip," Leonard said. "Didn't know that they still grew girls like her."

"I'll give that marriage a month," Dolores declared. "Maybe less."

The next day, Dolores gave James the keys to the old house, and Leonard hired Zola as a model. After two weeks on their honeymoon, James got a job with the law firm of Zimmerman and Lowe, and Zola started working in the shop. One day, a buyer came in and purchased several dresses and furs. Zola made the sale, and when the client wanted a model to deliver them to his suite, she took it upon herself to deliver them.

Later that evening, James called the house. "Zola is not home. Are you working her late?"

"Her hours are not this late," Dolores informed him. "Call Julienne."

3 o'clock that morning, James called from the police station. "I found Zola at the Hilton Hotel. I punched the client. Can you bail me out of jail?"

Leonard phoned the shop's lawyer and followed him to the police station. "You're lucky the client didn't' t want to press charges."

"Yeah, sure! He just didn't want this wife to know that he was with another woman." James looked like a dog that had been whipped and sent to the corner of the room to lick his wounds. His initial shock and the pain of betrayal had been replaced by anger and fear that Zola would do it again.

After that incident, James and Zola's marriage was steadily dissolving. They couldn't stand being in the same room, and she continued going out with the clients and getting home early in the morning. Then one night, after Leonard and Dolores had gone to bed, the phone rang. Leonard answered to hear Zola sobbing. "H-e-l-p me___"

"Zola? Where are you?"

"Somewhere near the docks, under a bridge, the east river," she whimpered. "Come and get me. I'm afraid."

"Hold on. We're coming." Leonard called for Herman and he and Dolores hurried to the car, in their pajamas and robe. Herman drove fast and made it in forty-five minutes. They jumped out of the car and ran to Zola's side. She was standing there, holding her clothing to cover her bare breast "What happened," Dolores asked, wide eyed and with an open mouth.

"I went out with a buyer to some club. We danced and had fun till he got drunk and acted a fool."

"Why didn't you leave," Dolores asked, shaking her head.

"The bastard wouldn't let me. Just held me and kept on drinking," she said, sobbing. "When we did leave, he drove like a damn mad man. Then stopped under this bridge and tried to remove my clothes."

Leonard breathed hard through his nose and shook his head as he gazed at how disheveled her hair and clothing appeared. "How did you get away from him?"

"I struggled and I kicked, and, then, I___" she started crying, pursed her lip and glanced at Dolores. "I feel violated."

"What did you expect?" Dolores said, eyeing her with contempt. "Sashaying around with half your tits hanging out."

"Don't speak to me that way, old woman. After what I've been through__." She started sobbing again, pursed her lips and breathing in and out loudly through her nose. "You never liked me from day one."

Dolores snapped at her," Maybe I would have if you had shown some class."

Leonard saw that the argument was getting heated and he said, rather sharply, surveying the area around them, "Let's get out of here. This isn't the safest part of town." He hurried them to the car, and Herman sped of. By the time the car had pulled into the driveway of the old house, Zola was feeling a little better, and had stopped crying.

"Home. Safe and sound," Leonard said.

"Thanks, Leonard," Zola said and started to open the car door.

"Stay put. Help her out and to the front door, Herman."

"Yes, sir," he said, getting out, helping her and averting his eyes, trying not to gaze at her. After that night, Dolores and Zola didn't have much to say to each other. She continued to work at the shop, but never again went out with any of the buyers. This lasted a year until one night; she left a note for James. A buyer had promised to get a top paying modeling job for her, and she ran off with him.

Good riddance," Dolores said. "She was an embarrassment to the shop and to this family."

Later that evening, after Dolores had finished consoling James, Michelle phoned. She was excited about a young man whom she had met. "We've a lot in common," she said. "I don't think I'll ever want to come home again."

"Be careful," Dolores warned. "Don't let him break your heart."

"I'm always careful," she said, sounding happy. When Dolores was done talking with Michelle, she and Leonard were about to have dinner when the doorbell rang. Jenny answered and showed Sonny into the dining room. Leonard invited him to sit and eat with them. The three of them sat at the dinner table, in the smaller of the family's two dining rooms. Sonny started a conversation. "I'm going to Paris tomorrow. I've gotta' check out this guy Michelle says she's crazy about."

"Michelle is smart," Dolores said. "She is nobody's fool."

"Yeah? James is too, but he got took. I'm not going to let her make the same mistake."

"How are you going to handle this?" She asked, thinking about the repercussions of any action he would take. "You know how she protects her independence."

"I'll think of some way to handle it when I get there. We've become pretty close. She'll listen."

Dolores and Leonard smiled at each other, and then glanced away. Dolores found herself wondering if she and Leonard could ever become friends with Sonny. The kids had made him a part of their life by giving him a second chance, and maybe they should take a chance on him too. They sat there talking about their kids, and the night grew long.

"I'd better get home and start packing. I'm leaving early tomorrow," Sonny said.

Three days later, Dolores and Leonard were about to leave for work when Michelle phoned. "Daddy has ruined everything. I'll never see Eugene again."

"Calm down, Michelle. Just what exactly did your daddy do?"

"He found Eugene in my bedroom," she answered, sounding furious. "He said that my conduct was unbecoming of a lady."

"What about Eugene?"

"Daddy made him leave," she said, angrily.

Sounds like Sonny's unannounced visit had thrown everything into a tailspin, Dolores thought. "You're really angry with your daddy, aren't you?"

"Darn right I am. He overreacted."

Sonny was remembering what he would have done in a room with a young lady, Dolores thought. The things he did to her, she had never dared dream of, filling her with a desire so powerful that she always wanted more. When it came to overpowering you sexually, he was an expert.

Michelle was more mature, not like her when she was younger, and she was ready to believe her when she said that nothing happened with her and Eugene, but she didn't want to undermine Sonny yet. "Don't be too angry with your daddy. He thought that he was doing what was best."

"How would he know?" She said. "He doesn't know what's best for him."

"He loves you and James. You kids are all he has."

"I know, Mom, but I love Eugene."

"Who is this Eugene?"

"Eugene Glauert."

Dolores felt a sharp pain in her head. Was her hearing impaired? "Did you say Glauert? Didn't I warn you to stay away from them?"

"Gees, you're as bad as Daddy. I'm twenty-one. I'll decide who is right and who is wrong for me."

"We don't like those Glauert's and they don't like us."

"Aw, Mom, this is the twentieth century. No one pays attention to family feuds."

This was the first time Michelle had spoken to her in that manner, but she sounded independent, not rebellious, and it made her remember the times she had fought with Mama Kate.

"You haven't met Eugene. Already, you've condemned him."

Dolores' heart sank and she became worried. Michelle could tell her to go to hell, which was certain to happen, if she and Sonny pushed her too hard. It was her life, and she was going to do exactly what she wanted to do; just as you did, she told herself. "I'll come to Paris, meet this__ Eugene, who has stolen your heart."

"Fair enough," she said.

When Dolores finished talking with Michelle, she told Leonard about their conversation. He was all for putting the situation into some perspective. "We need a break. Let's get a flight tomorrow." Dolores and Leonard packed their luggage that night, and took an early flight the next morning. When they arrived in Paris, Sonny met them at Orly Airport. "I'm staying at the Ritz. It's two blocks past the luxury shops of the Rue de la Paix."

"Maybe we should stay there instead of the chateau," Dolores said. "I wouldn't want Michelle to think that we're monitoring her."

Leonard rejected that idea, "No. We'll live at the chateau. It's large enough for us to keep our distance."

When Dolores, Leonard and Sonny arrived at the chateau, Michelle was waiting for them. They hugged and kissed her, then got settled to relax after their long flight. Two hours later, Michelle came to their room to talk. "Eugene is the son of Joliet Glauert. Philip Glauert is his cousin."

"I seem to remember Philip mentioning his father's brother, Joliet." Leonard said. "When can we meet your Eugene?"

"Tonight. He's coming to dinner."

"I had better get the cook started on the menu," Dolores said. "Angeletta? Prepare something light." She knew from her past experience that French meals consisted of a number of simple, superbly prepared dishes, served in small, light courses. You could eat a lot and get up from the table feeling light. She hurried for the kitchen and gave the menu to the cook. "We will have grilled beef, sliced thin, roast chicken, calves liver, cheese omelets, and exquisite legumes."

"Yes, Madame."

"Don't put any creamy or oily sauces on the vegetables, and serve a rose' wine with the dinner," Dolores recommended.

Around 6 o'clock, everyone was dressed and waiting in the family room for Eugene to arrive. When the doorbell rang, Emalia, the maid, answered and told Eugene to go to the family room, since he already was familiar with the chateau. Leonard and Sonny stood when he entered, and Michelle made the introductions. "Eugene, meet my step-father, Leonard Velasco. You've met Daddy, and this is my Mom, Mrs. Dolores Velasco."

Dolores gazed at him. Quite handsome, she thought. He doesn't resemble any of the Glauert's she had met. His complexion was a shade darker than the other Glauerts, his eyes more slanted, a pug nose and wavy hair. He stood five inches taller than Michelle's five feet four inches. She was about to shake his hand, but he took her by her shoulders and kissed both of her cheeks, the French traditional greeting.

Eugene talked about his family; "Poppa manages his fabric mill at Posset, outside the woods at Saint-Germain-en Laye." He smiled, revealing dimples in both cheeks, and pearly white teeth. "Mother helps. She designs all types of materials."

"Was your mother born in Paris?" Dolores asked.

"Poppa met and married her in Latin America. She's Brazilian."

"Then you must be fluent in Spanish," Dolores said.

"Si', Senora Velasco."

They talked for an hour before Angeletta announced, "Dinner is served, Madame."

Dolores and Leonard seemed to like Eugene. They were talking and laughing throughout dinner. Michelle seemed pleased that they were getting along so well. After dinner, they had wine in the family room and talked more about Eugene's family. It was known that the Glauert family considered his father an outcast because his father had selected a wife outside of their bourgeoisie clan, and because of this, they were not close.

After several hours of interesting conversation, Eugene said goodnight.

"It was a great evening," Leonard said, watching Eugene leave.

"I like the man," Sonny admitted. "I misjudged him."

"I'm happy to hear you say that Daddy, because he has asked me to marry him and I have accepted."

"That's my daughter. She's always known what she wanted," Dolores declared and hugged her.

"Congratulations!" Leonard said and kissed her cheek. "He seems like a fine young man."

"Yeah, fine looking and a stud," Sonny remarked. "You've made the right choice." He put his arms around her. "Forgive your old man for doubting you?"

"Of course, Daddy. I'm expecting you and Leonard to give me away. I can't choose one of you over the other."

"That's going to look odd," Dolores said. "Two fathers of the bride?"

"I do have two Fathers," Michelle stated. "How lucky can a girl get?"

After shopping for a week, and trying to get everything done, exactly as Michelle wanted, the wedding day had finally arrived. The Velasco and the Brown family were trying to get ready on time to arrive at the American Pro-Cathedral of the Holy Trinity Church for the wedding. Leonard, James and Sonny had their own Valet to help them to get dressed, and Michelle and Dolores had a maid. After several hours, they were finally ready. Leonard and Sonny had rented four Mercedes for their family and friends.

When they had arrived at the church, the news reporters and photographer rushed toward them as they exited their cars and nearly blinded them with their flash bulbs. Dolores rushed Michelle into the church rectory to get her away from the crowd. The wedding participants had thirty minutes to take their places in the church entrance.

Leonard and Sonny were waiting to march Michelle down the aisle, Sonny on her right and Leonard on her left.

"You look gorgeous, Daughter," Leonard said.

"Foxy like her mama," Sonny said, showing nearly, all thirty-two teeth.

Michelle had chosen a short, white, satin dress, slim fitted with pearls and tiny diamonds on the bodice and sleeves. A small crown with a veil adorned her head and a long train that extended two feet. She carried lily of the valley and white nosegays.

Six brides-maids wore Aqua taffeta dresses trimmed in white, a Tierra of small, white roses and bouquets of white roses with one red rose in the center. The brides-maids' escorts wore a light blue tuxedo, black bow tie and red coronations in their lapel.

The ring bearer wore a white suit, aqua cummerbund and a bow tie to match. Five flower girls wore short, white, laced dresses with wide hoops and crinoline slips, an aqua sash, socks and ribbons to match.

The reception was held at La Tete De L'Art, a very fancy joint, which is always filled with Parisian celebrities, because of their delicious food. Everyone was having a great time, especially Joliet; he was dancing with the maiden who caught the bridal bouquet. The festivities lasted for two hours, and then, Michelle and Eugene flew to Aruba for their honeymoon.

Chapter Nine

That Morning, after Michelle and Eugene's wedding, James, Leonard and Dolores were sleeping late, and were awakened by the phone. Analoude Glauert, Eugene's mother, was inviting them for brunch. They got up, dressed, and went to the Glauert's mansion. They sat at the table smiling at each other. Analoude broke the silence, "We're fortunate to have gained a daughter, you and another son," she said in her native accent.

Dolores thought Analoude was stylish sitting in her burnish red and gold dashiki, small golden hoops in her ears and three large gold bracelets on her left arm. She must have been all of sixty, but her excellent bone structure had retained its youthful shape and her oval face was as smooth as vanilla pudding. When she smiled, her green eyes merrily lit up like a brilliance of emeralds.

"Let's hold hands and say the blessing," she suggested.

"It's awkward holding hands at a table for twenty people when there are only five of us seated." Joliet said, his carefree blue eyes penetrating hers. He reached across the table and his jazzy blue silk tie almost fell into the creamed potatoes. "Wow," he said, and critically examined his tie.

He seemed to have exotic taste for colors, Dolores thought, eyeing his rust colored suit. It did match his sun-tanned complexion and brown windblown hair. He loosened his tie and unbuttoned his shirt a bit, revealing his thick muscular neck. He was well built but trim of figure with long legs and much better looking than his brother, Jacques'.

Analoude paid little attention to what was happening with Joliet and began the prayer, "Today is precious to us, Lord. Our children have joined us as one. We rejoice in your blessings, Amen."

The evening went along smoothly as Leonard talked about his shops, and Joliet' talked about his fabric mill. Dolores felt that she had much in common with Analoude, seeing that they both coordinated their husband's business.

After spending two hours with the Glauerts, they went home to pack, and later that evening, got a flight to New York. Herman met them at the airport. When they arrived home, Dolores headed for the bathroom. "Jacuzzi, here I come. I want to soak and then go to bed."

Leonard laughed and followed her. "I have something that will perk you up."

"Mr. Velasco, you dirty old man." She pushed him into the bathroom. She realized that she wasn't as tired as she had thought, and that Leonard was still quite a lover.

The next morning, everyone was back to his or her usual routines. Dolores found herself in the middle of more decisions, "Swimwear is fashionable this year. I'm thinking of adding it to our collection."

"It's your baby. Run with it," Leonard said.

Dolores was once again ordering material and approving sketches, and working her designers at odd hours past the workday. One evening, while working late, she had decided to stop for dinner at K-Paul's. James was seated with a group, and he had his arms around a beautiful woman. Dolores went over and stood in front of them.

"Mom, what are you doing here?" A smile, almost as wide as the Hudson River, lit his face.

"I'm working late. What are you doing here?" She waited for him to introduce the young lady, and she didn't move, and didn't blink, waiting for him to say something.

"Christy, my Mom, Dolores Velasco," he finally said.

Christy turned her large blue eyes toward her and said, in a soft, sweet voice, "Hi, Mrs. Velasco." Her blue taffeta dress was almost the color of her eye, and she wore it with perfection. Her high yellow complexion was blemish free. She had full breast, a tiny waist and shoulder length blond hair that was impeccably coffered. Dolores could tell that she was sophisticated by her manner of dress. Her blue taffeta dress fitted simply, not too loose or tight fitting, discreet pearls in her ears, a bracelet to match and a pearl ring on her right index finger. "Sit with us," she said, extending her hand to Dolores, causing the large diamond on her ring finger to sparkle from the light in the restaurant.

"Are you two engaged?" Dolores asked, feeling stupid for asking.

"Sorry, you've found out this way, Mom," James said. I was hoping to tell you and Leonard this weekend."

"When is the wedding," she asked, still feeling hurt.

"This spring," Christy answered. "I could use your expertise about fashion."

Dolores felt a little better and could see that not only did this girl have class but finesse. "It will be my pleasure."

The wedding was scheduled for April and by March, Dolores and Christy were overwhelmed, between ordering material for her wedding gown, fittings, keeping track of wedding gifts and bridal showers given by friends.

Finally, April arrived, and a beautiful wedding was held in the Trinity Church at Broadway and Wall Streets. Christy wore white China Silk, with a ten-foot train, and a white silk veil attached to a pearl crown. Eight bridesmaids and four flower girls look beautiful in their lavender colored satin dresses. James and the escorts wore a black tuxedo and matching trousers, stiff white shirts with attached collar, black bow tie and black cummerbund. The ring bearer wore a white suit with a black bow tie. Sonny and Leonard wore an Oxford gray cutaway coat with gray striped trousers, pearl tray waistcoat, stiff white shirt, stiff fold-down collar, and four-in-hand black-and-gray tie.

Dolores chose to wear a rose—colored brocade evening gown with satin shoes to match.

The reception was held at the Waldorf-Astoria. The chefs there did a great job preparing the delicious food. There were four hundred guest and music by Bob James that lasted until midnight.

Michelle, Eugene, Analoude, Joliet', Leonard and Dolores took Christy and James to the airport for their flight to Barbados. On their way back home, Michelle announced that she was pregnant.

Tears filled Dolores' eyes the moment she heard the news. "I'm going to be a grandmother."

Sonny kissed Michelle and felt her stomach. "Please take care of yourself and my grandson."

"Who said that it's a boy?" Leonard asked. "I'd like to have a granddaughter."

"Whatever," Dolores said. "We'll be happy as grandparents."

When Michelle and Eugene went back to Paris, Dolores phoned every month to see how she was doing.

"It's no difficult pregnancy, but I'm in the bathroom every morning retching my insides out," Michelle said. "Everything makes me nauseous."

"Try and hold on," Dolores advised. "Your nausea will soon past. Eat a lot of crackers. No salt"

Several months later, during early morning hours of January, Michelle went into labor. Eugene called Dolores and Leonard from the lobby of the American Hospital. "We have a little girl, born thirty minutes ago. She's beautiful; curly black hair with a single curl on top like a pixie."

Dolores and Leonard were anxious to see the baby. They made reservations on the next flight out, and phoned Sonny to let him know, only to find that he had already left.

When Dolores and Leonard landed at Orly, they headed for the hospital. Michelle was sitting up in bed, when they got to her room. "Congratulations!" Dolores yelled and held her in her arms. You look wonderful."

Michelle's hair was pulled back behind her ears and held with a pink ribbon to match her lace gown. Her face was still chubby. She laughed and asked, "Wonderful? You're kidding. I've gained thirty pounds."

"You're beautiful," Leonard said and kissed her. "You've made us grandparents."

"They're bringing her for her feeding, in a few minutes. You'll get to see her."

No sooner had she spoken, the nurse entered and handed the baby to Michelle. She smiled down at her daughter and turned to her mama. "Want to hold her?" she asked, putting the baby in Dolores' arms.

"She's such a beauty." Dolores held her close. "What's her name?"

"Eugene named her Sherrie."

Dolores passed the baby to Leonard. He kissed the baby's forehead, and was about to give her to Michelle when Sonny entered the room.

"Wait! Give her to me." He took the baby, walked around the room and started whispering to her. "Were you waiting for your grandpa?"

"Be careful," Leonard said, following behind him.

Michelle held out her arms. "That's enough, Daddy, she's hungry. Bring her to me." She took the baby, pulled out an engorged breast and offered it to her. She nursed noisily and greedily on the milk, making all kinds of funny little noises.

They all laughed and Sonny said, "That girl can put away some food. I bet she'll want to eat all the time."

After a couple of days, Michelle and the baby went home.

"I can't wait to take care of Sherrie," Dolores said.

"I'm going shopping," Sonny announced, hurrying out of the door.

"Wait for me," Leonard ran behind him.

When Sherrie was a week old, Sonny and Leonard bought dozens of toys. They wanted to see who was going to spoil her the most, and were like two little kids waiting to play with the new kid on the block. They both proudly displayed the toys that they had bought by laying them all out on the floor next to Sherrie.

"Everything you bought is too advanced for Sherrie," Dolores said.

"Don't matter," Sonny said. "I'll show her how to use them when she's older."

Eugene had hired a nanny to take care of Sherrie and she wanted to keep her on a schedule of feedings and nap time. Sonny and Leonard didn't like the schedule. They were bent on spoiling her. "Leonard and I are going to make a schedule that everyone can abide by," Sonny said.

Neither of them slept that night, and the baby cried more than she had the day before. The nanny was up five times to care for Sherrie, and she was not happy with Sonny and Leonard.

Five months later, Sherrie had gotten her lower central incisors. Leonard and Sonny took turns taking pictures of her. A month later, they had her on the floor, trying to teach her to crawl.

"They've visited second childhood," Dolores said. She and Michelle sat nearby, watching, laughing and making fun of them.

"I'm sure Sherrie doesn't know what to make of all of this," Michelle said.

The nanny won't have to put up with this much longer," Dolores said. "We all have to get back to our businesses."

"I don't want you to go." Michelle pursed her lips sadly. "It's nice having my family here."

"I don't want to go either. Hopefully we can return Christmas."

Dolores and Leonard were getting ready for their anniversary party. She danced about, inspecting everything that Jenny had done. "This gray linen, pink napkins and pink coronation centerpiece is saying something with this Limoges china."

"Yes, Ma'am, just like you ordered." Sounding pleased that Dolores was satisfied with what she had done.

"Our guest will be here at 7:30. Where's that bartender?"

"The party room. Waiting for your instructions."

Dolores' voice was resounding, but she didn't mean to hurt Jenny's feelings. "Why didn't you say something?" She turned on her heels and hurried to the party room. The bartender had started pouring the drinks. "You're prompt, Mr.__?"

"Willie, Ma'am."

"Ok, Willie, I've got two cases of champagne in the cellar."

An hour later, after making sure everything was ready, Dolores went upstairs to get dressed. Jenny had laid her blue, silk gown and blue-white diamond necklace on the bed. Leonard entered the room, held her for a moment and kissed her. "Hi, sweet. Looks like you've got everything under control, as usual."

"I had to get this one right. We've had eighteen blissful years of marriage."

"This is going to be some party," he said, getting into his tuxedo.

They had just finished dressing when the doorbell rang. They descended the stairs holding hands and stood by the stairs while Jenny opened the door. Four couples of the seventy-five guests invited, entered the foyer. Leonard greeted them, "Betty__Sam, good to see you. Hello, Stanley, Erica, you're looking beautiful as ever. Come in Bill__Dottie. This way Bob." He put his arm around Bob's wife, Marie, and led her to the party room with the others.

The trio, Leonard had engaged for the evening, began playing as everyone took a seat. They had begun to dance when the others started arriving and soon joined the fun. Dolores whispered to Leonard, "Our party is jumping."

"Yes," He agreed. "No one is going home tonight."

Later in the evening, Michelle, Eugene, James and Christy arrived when the dinner was being served "Happy anniversary, Mom, Leonard," they said in unison. They sat at one of the party tables that had been rented to accommodate seventy-five guests.

After dinner, Dolores and Leonard opened their gifts to each other. Leonard took her hand, kissed it, reached into his pocket and withdrew a large, beautiful ruby ring surrounded by a circle of blue-white diamonds. "Happy anniversary, sweet." He slipped the ring on her finger, and she was mesmerized.

"I love it." She planted kisses over his face.

He laughed and pulled her into his arms. "No joke. You like it?"

"Try taking it from me." She held the ring up to the light watching its brilliance. Then she opened her gift to him and placed a gold watch on his wrist. "You're my sunshine and my moonlight. You complete my life."

"All right, Mom," James said, clapping his hands. "Why can't you say something like that to me, Christy?"

"We haven't been married as long." She answered with a defensive note in her voice.

"What's that got to do with anything?" Eugene said with a frown slashing his brow.

Christy put her hands on her hips, her eyes shifted back and forth from Eugene to Michelle and she shot back at him, "I don't hear Michelle making any declarations."

Michelle reached for Eugene's hand, placed it in hers and held their entwined fingers toward Christy. "We're in this love together, forever!" Then she winked at her, pulled him to her and kissed his lips passionately.

Christy relented. "Ok, you two. I got the message." She went over to James, pulled him into her arms and kissed him, sucking his breath into her mouth.

He came up gasping for air. "Wow! You got me started, woman. Let's continue this upstairs."

She followed him to the stairs, looked back at Michelle and winked.

"You work it, girlfriend," Michelle said.

The guest had left. Dolores, Leonard and Sonny sat and talked. Leonard was sipping a martini and talking about Sherrie. Then, Sonny started mimicking Sherrie eating. Leonard laughed so hard that he got strangled on his drink, and fell back in his chair gasping for breath.

Dolores slapped his back, and his mouth twisted, his eyes rolled back and he clutched his arm.

"Call 911," Sonny said, rushing to his side.

Michelle screamed and ran to the phone. "Ambulance, please." she cried into the phone, her voice trembling. "My Father is having a heart attack."

Within minutes, the paramedics arrived and before wheeling Leonard into the ambulance, gave him cardiopulmonary resuscitation and kept him on Oxygen. He was placed in intensive care.

Dolores sobbed silently, and Sonny took her into his arms to comfort her. "Let me take you home. We can come back tomorrow."

"No." She pushed him away. "I'm staying."

"Then, I'm staying too." He took her into his arms again.

She went to Leonard's bedside, kissed him and felt his forehead. "Cold and clammy. He's only fifty-two." She formed the praying hands with her hands. "Please, God, don't take him from me. Let him pull through." Their life together flashed before her eyes. They had lived a rich, beautiful life together, but she wanted more. She bent over him and placed a wet kiss on his brow. She stayed with him, talking to him, praying and hoping he would regain consciousness, especially after the doctor had assured her that he wasn't brain dead.

On the second night, Leonard stirred, looked at Dolores and mumbled, "Remember the times we had together? That day we got married made me the happiest man alive."

"Honey, don't talk." She got in bed beside him. "Save your strength."

He continued, weakly. "I love you for honoring me by becoming my wife."

"Shush, rest my darling. We will have more wonderful days again."

Leonard died that night. Dolores stayed next to him, sobbing silently with Sonny trying to console her. "Let' go, babe it's all over. You'll make yourself sick."

James and Sonny helped her out to the car, and they sat, holding her.

"He loved Paris." Dolores had Leonard's body flown to Paris. On the day of the funeral, a long line of cars followed the cortege from the cathedral and through the square off Boulevard Des Capucines to the gravesite on a high hill overlooking a vast meadow, where he was laid to rest.

Dolores wanted to be alone, but Michelle wouldn't let her. "Come, Mom, you're going home with me."

"I'd rather stay at the chateau. I want to be alone with my memories."

"Not this time." Michelle took her arm and guided her to her car. "You can stay there later."

Dolores went along, unwillingly, feeling numb, lost and bewildered. The next day, she moped around her room in her gown, not getting dressed until dinnertime. It was like this everyday for six months. Then one morning, she refused to get out of bed. "Mom is in a state," Michelle said. "She sleeps too much."

"We have to do something," Eugene said. "But what?"

"Maybe Daddy can help her," Michelle suggested, going to the phone to call him.

Thirty minutes later, Sonny was by Dolores' side. "What's wrong, babe?"

She kept her back to him and spoke in an inaudible voice, "I have nothing and no one left.

He went around to her side of the bed. "Look at me," he demanded.

Her eyes slowly met his, he smiled and she gave him a slight smile before her face crumpled into tears. "I miss him so." She dabbed her eyes with a big yellow handkerchief. "He was like the air that I breathe."

"I know you miss him, babe. You're forty-two and a beautiful woman who's got a lot of living to do." He gently patted her cheeks. "The family and I need you."

She stopped crying and he heard fear in her voice. "I don't want to be alone."

"You're not alone." He bent down and kissed her lips."

She raised her body slowly and sat on the side of the bed, and he sat next to her with his arm around her waist. "Who's running the stores in New York?"

"James is helping me."

"Don't you think Leonard would want you on the job?"

"You're right." She blew her nose loudly. "I have to get back to our business."

"We can leave when you're ready," he said.

"Tonight. I want to leave tonight."

After Sonny left, Dolores rushed to pack her luggage. Everything was ready, she thought, until she sat before the mirror. "My face! My hair." She hurried to the phone to call Raphael's Beauty Salon.

Later that night, Dolores and Sonny said their goodbyes to Michelle, Sherrie and Eugene, and then left for New York. Herman met them at Kennedy Airport. Dolores was in a somber mood, and Sonny didn't say anything until Herman drove into her driveway. "Want me to stay tonight?"

"If you behave," she answered, hoping that he would. She was in no mood to wrestle with him.

"You have my word. I'll go quietly into the guest room." He gave the scouts honor and grinned.

"Sonny, I know that look. Just in case you decide to sleepwalk, I'm going to keep a bat under the covers with me."

"Come on, babe, you think I'd do that to you after all you've been through?" He gave her a serious glance. "Love is more than sex." He blew a kiss to her and went to his room.

Dolores slept soundly until the sun, shining brightly on her face, awakened her. She got out of bed, opened the window, and inhaled the cool breeze that rushed over her. She closed her eyes and thought of Leonard, how he used to stand there and inhale the fresh morning air. Then she heard a light tap on her door. "One minute." She got back in bed.

Sonny entered and stood beside her bed looking down on her, wanting her, and aching for her. He started to touch her but withdrew his hand. "The weather is great outside. Let's have breakfast downtown and spend the whole day in the park."

"No way! I have to get to work."

"Come on. James can take care of everything for one day longer." He took her hands and pulled her out of the bed and into his arms. Her low cut, sheer nightgown revealed her ample bosom and other bodily dimensions.

"Sonny!" She exclaimed and jumped back into bed. "You're stretching it."

"Sorry," He said, grinning. "I'm hungry."

"Please leave so that I can get dressed." She gave him an inexorable look.

A sly smile snaked around the corners of his down turned mouth. "Ok. I'll wait downstairs."

They had breakfast at Don's, and later, a picnic in the park. After lunch, Dolores had decided that she'd had enough. "I want to go home."

"No. You need rest. Let's go to Fire Island, take a ferry boat ride along Barrier Beach."

She went along and stuck it out, waiting for the ride to end. When they got back to shore, Sonny bought a bottle of wine, and when they arrived home, he poured two glasses and handed one to her.

"Sonny, really? Chardonnay?" She wrinkled her nose.

"I know, but it'll perk you up. Get your blood flowing."

"No thanks. I'll have champagne." She got up to go to the bar and he quickly blocked her path, pulled her into his arms and slowly ran the tip of his tongue erotically over her lips.

She gasped and struggled, like a tiger, to free herself. "Do that again and I'll__."

"You'll what?" He interrupted, showing her his old charm. He laughed, backed away and asked, "When are you going to accept that there's a reason why I can't keep my hands off you?"

She stared at him without cracking a smile, trying to ignore the sensation his kiss had ignited. Although she blamed him for the way that he was acting, she couldn't excuse herself for being just as eager as he was. Her body had wanted what her mind had told her was wrong. She was still vulnerable when he was around and she had to put a stop to his nonsense. "Am I going to have to put you out?"

"No," he quickly said. "I remember the last time you put me out."

She kept her gaze on him. The years had not lessened the effect he had on her. Though she tried to forget, she thought him to be more desirable than ever. Oh, God! Leonard's grave is still fresh, and here she was letting Sonny thrill her. Her eyes filled with tears.

"You've got to let it go, babe."

"I'm trying."

"Try harder." He took his handkerchief and wiped her eyes. "Leonard would want you to."

"You don't know what it's like. You haven't lost anyone."

"I lost you. That was just as bad."

"I don't want to talk about it." She backed away. "I'm going to bed." She went to her room, leaving him standing in the middle of the room.

The next morning, Dolores got out of bed early and went to work. Her staff greeted her with smiles and hugs, and for a brief moment, she was her old self again, delegating her authority, ushering everyone back to work and delving right in the middle of it herself.

One evening, after she had gotten home, she found Sonny waiting on her front porch. He was all excited.

"Michelle had a baby boy."

Dolores packed a few clothing and made reservations for the next flight to Paris. Sonny did the same and they sat together on the flight. "Wonder what she'll name the baby?" Sonny asked.

"Most likely, he'll have Eugene's name."

"James should have been named after me."

She shot up in her seat. "Why, after twenty-six years, you have to say that now?" She stared at him, then rolled her eyes upward. "You never said anything after he was born."

"I was only eighteen. Didn't know no better."

"Well, it's too late now." She turned and stared out of the window.

"Don't be angry, babe, I wasn't blaming you."

"That's what you implied."

"No. I was just thinking of what could've been."

When the plane landed at Orly, they took a taxi to the American Hospital. Eugene was with Michelle and he was holding the baby. Dolores and Sonny rushed over to him. "Let me hold my grandson," Dolores said, smiling.

"He's a handsome little dude," Sonny said, looking down on him. "What is his name?"

"Same as mine," Eugene said, proudly.

Sonny hugged him and stated, "You're a lucky man." He went over to Michelle and kissed her cheeks. "Congratulations, Daughter. You've immortalized us."

"Thanks, Daddy, I had an easier time. He came into this world like a champ."

When Michelle and the baby left the hospital, Dolores and Sonny stayed three weeks before returning to New York. She was busier than ever, and had decided to add a new line of fashions for men. She hired several male models, along with a new set of rules. "No dating on the job. What you do after work is ok, but any scandal and you're fired."

One evening, when she was getting ready for a fashion show, she happened to glance out into the audience. "Blake?" She called from the stage, and motioned for him to come to the dressing room. He hurried toward he entrance, his eyes on her only, and she rushed into his arms. "How long have you been here?"

"A couple of minutes. Heard plenty about your fashions." He drew her closer into his arms. "You've got a lot of people working for you."

"Leonard had a hundred and fifty models when he started. Now we have twice that many."

"Impressive! I'm proud of you."

A few of the models rushed past them, interrupting their conversation. It was five o'clock, and the first time she had ever held a show during evening hours. "I've got to start the show. Wait for me when it's over." She gave him a kiss and hurried to get into what she would wear. A few minutes later, she stepped on stage wearing a cream suit with a beige weskit.

Each model appeared on stage before the audience, down a ramp that swirled into an S-shape around the seats. The crowd went wild with applause, whistles and approval. She took a bow and whispered toward the ceiling, "Leonard, we've done it again. The show was a success." She took several more bows and ended the show with a promise to have more of the same fashions in the coming months.

When she went back stage, Blake was waiting for her. "Let's have dinner and relax with a few drinks," he suggested.

"I must go home and change."

"You look great," he said. "You haven't changed since last we met." He kept staring at her as he led her out of the building and into his car. "What about some garlic shrimp or some good old spareribs?"

"Lead on, my dear. I'm with you."

Blake's chauffeur took them to Jezebel's on 530 Ninth Avenue. They ordered a combination of shrimp, spareribs and fried chicken. "Remember the times we spent together?"

"How can I forget? You were just as exciting then as you are now."

It was midnight when they left the restaurant. "The effects of the day has taken a toll on me. I'm tired and I'm high from the champagne," she admitted, with her head on his shoulder.

"Want me to tuck you in bed when we get home?"

"You sly devil!" She hit him on the arm fondly. "You haven't changed a bit."

The car pulled into her driveway and she slid out quietly. He unlocked her door and stood in the foyer for a moment,

"Quiet, isn't it?" She said. "Worst than the sound of noise." Tears slid down her face, and an overwhelming sensation of emptiness swept over her.

Blake seemed to have felt it too, and for the first time since he had known her, he was at a loss for words to console her. So he held her tightly in his arms. "Do you want me to stay tonight?"

"Thanks, but I will be fine. Tonight was great." She kissed him and walked him to the door.

For several weeks, Dolores and Blake saw a lot of each other. He was charming, attentive, and witty, and she enjoyed his company. He kissed her often, but not as deep and meaningful as before when he had asked her to marry him. It seemed that he had an obligation to his dead friend. He had promised him to take care of his wife. After their last date, Dolores knew that they would never be more than just friends. She came home, lay in bed and ran her hand over Leonard's side of the bed. "I miss you, honey," she murmured. Several hours later, she was still awake, and when the alarm clock sounded that morning, she got up, hurriedly got dressed and went to work.

When she arrived at work, Julienne was voicing her opinion over the new rules. "Why not dinner, one drink and a little night life with the male models? Is this slavery time?"

"Do what you want, but it had better not fall back on this store."

Julienne yawned loudly and Dolores came down on her, "You're not a bad looking woman, but you're no longer a spring chicken."

"What do you mean?" A spark of anger lit her eyes.

"Meaning, in this business, you're too old to start over."

Julienne stared at her as if she wanted to slap her, but instead, grabbed her purse and walked out.

It had been a rotten day. Dolores was a little upset because of the way she had to handle Julienne, and she just wanted to go home and get some sleep. After getting in bed and almost asleep, the phone rang. She answered, sleepily, "Yeah?"

"Hi, babe, did I wake you?"

"Sonny?"

"Sorry, babe, but I've been thinking about you. Can we have dinner tomorrow night?"

"Why didn't you ask me earlier?"

"Because____"

"Because what?"

"I don't know."

She snapped at him, "You're crazy, that's why. I have to get some sleep. See you tomorrow." She hanged the phone up and fell asleep as soon as her head hit the pillow.

The next morning, at work, Julienne was waiting in her office. "Alright." She was ringing her hands and pacing the floor. "I was wrong. Forgive me?"

Dolores hugged her and said, "You're still on board."

They laughed happily and walked arm in arm to the dressing room. They were about to plan the next fashion show when Sonny knocked on the door. "Could I see you a minute?" He opened the door without her permission.

She beckoned for him to come inside. "Excuse us, Julienne. What is it, Sonny?"

He took a seat and held her hand in his. "I love you, babe. I've spent half my life waiting for you." He drew her into his arms and kissed her lips. "Marry me."

She pushed him away, stared at him for a long moment, and threw him a rivaling question. "Why should I marry you?"

"We're both alone."

Her eyes searched his and she said, "You impossible fool. You'd better give me a better answer."

His mouth opened, his chest expanded, he drew in a quick breath and stated, "I haven't had a life since we parted, babe. I need you, but most of all, I love you." She didn't say anything, but thoughts went through her mind that were tantamount with what she felt in her heart. There was no one home to greet her at night, the warmth from the hot water bottle, in bed, didn't last all night, and she missed the intimacy with a man that brought her much pleasure. Sonny had been there for her when she needed someone, and he darn sure loved the family. She turned to him with a smile and said, "There's no need for us to be lonely."

A trace of pink crept into his face. I have loved you, woman, from the first moment I set eyes on you, and all the days of my life after our divorce. Please listen to me, babe__"

"You've convinced me," she said interrupting him, offering a slow smile and cutting her eyes at him.

"Babe, you'll do it?" He nearly choked on his words.

"Yeah! Now get out of here and let me get back to work."

"Not before I give you a sample of what you can expect from now on." He locked the door.

She swallowed hard as he unzipped his pants and stepped put of his briefs. Her heart began pounding. "Not here," she whispered, as he lay her gently on the sofa. She felt his hardness against her stomach and she shivered. Instantly she wanted him.

"I love the way you feel under my body." He kissed her throat, her soft yielding lips and probing tongue." He continued, running his tongue all over her breast. "I've thought of the way it felt when I first made love to you, how you accepted and matched everything I'd done to your body and how we melded together."

Never had he been as hard as this. She could no longer hold back the soft moan in her throat and she sounded like a kitten in heat as their bodies moved in unison so passionately and tenderly, yet hot and sensual. She came up, straining against him as he cupped his hands around her breast and sucked the nipple, and she let out a soft gasp of erotic joy when his mouth closed over the other nipple. She couldn't remember ever this much ecstasy as he plunged in and out, thrusting himself deeper within her, clutching her body to his until he exploded after she cried his name and he went limp. "This was a bad example for my models," she whispered, getting up and heading for the shower.

"Forget that. You're the boss," he said and joined her in the shower.

Fifteen minutes later, they got dressed and came out of the office smiling. "See you tonight" he said and kissed her.

When Dolores got home, Sonny had dinner and champagne on the table. "I told Michelle about us," he said. "She wants us to come to Paris. She is going to plan our wedding."

The thought of Michelle planning the wedding swelled Dolores' heart and she quickly said, "A Paris wedding would be different." She closed her eyes and imagined how she would look and what she would wear. "I'll get the designers to make my wedding dress."

Sonny kept talking, while Dolores dreamed, paying little attention to what either of them was saying until he mentioned when he expected them to get married, "It's got to be in two weeks."

"Sonny, that isn't enough time."

"Yes it is, babe. I can't wait much longer."

"Really, Sonny, I'm not running away or changing my mind." She was secretly thrilled by his reaction. "What difference would a month make?"

"Hell, woman, I can't stand another minute. After waiting all these years for you?"

Dolores had the designers working overtime, trying to get her dress finished, and after two weeks, she and Sonny were leaving for Paris. When they were on their way out of the door, the phone rang.

"Let it ring, babe. We have a plane to catch."

"Wait, Sonny, it may be important." She ran to answer and caught it on the last ring. "Blake! You're in town?"

Just got back from New Delhi. What about dinner tonight?"

She paused before answering, remembering the time she had to tell him that she was getting married. This time was different, but her heart rate rose for a moment, then returned to normal when she sucked in a deep breath, smiled and answered, "I'm on my way to Paris. Getting married tomorrow."

"Dejavou! Good luck this time, Dolores."

"Thanks, Blake." She put the phone back on the table. Sonny was standing silently behind her, She turned to face him and they stared into each other's eyes and smiled. They were going to be together again, and she knew without a doubt that this time, nothing would split them apart. He took her hand, helped her down the steps and into the car.

"Great day for flying, Herman said.

"Perfect," Dolores answered. "The forecast promised a bright, beautiful day."

"All your days will be bright and beautiful from now on, babe. I'll see to it personally."

Epilogue

All of Dolores and Sonny's heart aches and problems were well behind them. When they had boarded the airplane, buckled their seat belts and the sign had been turned off instructing them to silence their telephones, I Pads, and music, Dolores placed a call to Michelle. "I have an announcement to make. Your daddy wants to be married in two weeks."

Michelle laughed and said, "That's my Daddy. He wants everything when he wants it."

"I know. I know," Dolores said and laughed.

Sonny's face had turned red with emotion and he placed his hand over Dolores' where it rested on the arm- rest. He whispered into the phone, "I'll have the perfect wedding and the perfect wife. I expect all of you present and accounted for in the church."

"Did you hear that, Michelle?" Dolores asked.

"Yes, Mom. You and Daddy will have a beautiful Paris wedding."

"We'll see you when we get there," Dolores said.